ONE WELL-PLACED BULLET

Slocum brought his Winchester up slowly, not wanting to alert the marksman that he had been seen. Rolling on one hip, feeling the sharp edges of the stone scrape at his back and knees, he sighted slowly, almost casually. He saw the headband, the bead of his sight resting dead center on the red cloth, then raised it an inch, then two.

The bullet would drop a little, and Slocum wanted to make a point. He wanted to make sure. He tightened his finger on the trigger, held his breath . . . and squeezed. . . .

The Indian fell head downward. On the back of his shirt, there was a red stain clearly visible in the brilliant sunshine, then he plunged into shade and Slocum lost sight of him for a second.

He heard the dull thud of the body landing, not loud enough to echo. And it was silent again.

"That's one," Slocum mumbled.

OTHER BOOKS BY JAKE LOGAN

H.H.

JAKE LOGAN

SLOCUM AND THE APACHE RAIDERS

B

BERKLEY BOOKS, NEW YORK

SLOCUM AND THE APACHE RAIDERS

A Berkley Book / published by arrangement with
the author

PRINTING HISTORY
Berkley edition / April 1991

ISBN: 0-425-12659-5

10 9 8 7 6 5 4 3 2 1

1

John Slocum stood in the stirrups and watched the cloud of dust billow up against the wall of Broken Back Mesa. The ball of beige, certainly not smoke, drifted on a hot stiff breeze, angling toward the sharp edges of the notch which gave the mesa its name. Funneled through the deep cut, the dust squirmed like a headless snake as it stretched out into a long, winding column then disappeared among the boulders.

He tilted his hat back and dabbed at his forehead with a dusty kerchief. It was too damn hot to breathe, let alone work, but Vernon Settle didn't give a damn whether he breathed or not. Just do your work, that's what Settle wanted. That's what he paid you for, and he made no bones about it. Anything less than full days meant you got a week's wages and a kick in the butt. Not hard, but enough to get you moving to the next town or the one after that.

Slocum had worked for Settle for three months, and he knew the irascible old man better than he cared to. There was little to recommend Settle to the company of cowhands and wranglers, let alone polite society. He was hard as nails, mean as a snake and just about as deadly. But Vernon Settle was a fair man, for all that, and it suited Slocum just fine. He'd had worse jobs, lots of them, and this one hadn't been that easy to come by. So, when he saw the dust cloud, he knew he had better see what caused it. Because as Settle saw it, he'd sure as hell want to know.

Slocum had field glasses, government issue, and they hung around his neck like a reminder of just how much the South had lost. Every time he saw the damn things, he'd remember the war. His breath would catch in his throat a second, and he'd get just a faint hint of gunsmoke and, under the acrid stench, the sweeter smell of blood. When you lived through that, as Slocum had, running horses for an ill-tempered old abolitionist was a mixed blessing, but a blessing still.

Even through the glasses, Slocum couldn't see more than the dust. It rolled across the bone-dry floor of the valley, parallel to the foot of the mesa. Whatever was causing it was far enough away that the rising dust no longer got sucked into the notch. Instead, it seemed to spread out in a flat layer maybe fifty or sixty feet off the ground. It looked like a fine mist, not unlike that before a summer squall, in everything but color. But the yellow-brown haze had nothing to do with rain.

At the bottom of the roiling cloud, it was impossible to see anything. Based on the size of it, Slocum figured there had to be ten or twelve riders, maybe more. Halfway between the ridge he sat on and the base of Broken Back Mesa, Settle's men had accumulated nearly two hundred mustangs. The *barranca,* a circular wall of matted and interlaced mesquite and thornbush, would hold the horses indefinitely. But it wouldn't keep out anyone determined to get at the animals.

Looking back down the slope behind him, he spotted Curly Haines and Rick Hardee, driving a handful of ponies. He didn't want to alert the advancing horsemen with a gunshot to get Curly's attention, so he wheeled his mount and charged down the slope at a breakneck pace, alternately flailing his hat and swatting the flanks of his big roan.

Curly must have sensed something, because he reined in and started looking around. When he finally glanced uphill and saw Slocum charging down on him, he called to Rick and the two men headed toward him.

"What's up, Slocum?" Curly asked.

"Not sure. There's a bunch of riders heading toward the *barranca,* around a dozen at least, I think, probably more."

"It ain't Vernon. He's on the way back to the ranch."

"I couldn't get a look. Too much dust. But I think we better check it out."

"Check it out, hell. We better go head 'em off. Tell 'em what's what. We busted our asses near two weeks for them mustangs."

"Suppose it's Indians?" Rick said.

"Don't matter to me," Curly said. He leaned over to let go with a long yellow sluice of tobacco juice, then licked his ginger mustache dry. "Those horses are ours. Indians or no."

"Apaches ain't likely to agree with you, Curly," Rick said. His voice sounded tight, and it quavered a little.

Curly noticed and winked at Slocum. "Don't make no difference, Ricky. Apaches don't take scalps anyhow. Nothing to worry about." He spat again, then turned to Slocum. "Reckon you better lead the way, John."

Slocum nodded. He pulled the roan in a tight circle then gave it a quick squeeze with his knees. The horse responded with a sudden spurt up the hill, and broke into a full gallop within a half-dozen strides.

As Slocum reapproached the ridgeline, he could already see the boiling dust cloud spreading across the blue edge of the hill like a tea stain on a tablecloth. By the time he reached the crest, Curly was alongside him.

Slocum reined in. There was no need to point. Instead, he handed the binoculars to Curly and waited while the foreman scanned the valley floor. Still peering through the glasses, he said, "I make it fifteen or so. Takes a lot of horses to kick up that much dust. 'Course, there don't have to be that many men. Could be half that number pulling swing mounts."

"Apaches do that, don't they, Curly?" Rick called. He had reined in some ten or twelve yards below the ridgeline. Curly looked back down the hill at him, but didn't answer. Instead, he turned to Slocum, handed the glasses back, and asked, "What do you think, John?"

"Your call, Curly."

Haines nodded. "All right. Let's go see can we scare 'em off . . . whoever the hell they are." He looked pointedly at Hardee. "You ready, Rick?"

Hardee nodded. He wasn't happy about it, and he made no attempt to hide the fact. "You're the boss, Curly."

"Damn right." He kicked his mount and started down the slope in front of him. The cloud of dust was more than halfway to the *barranca* now, and the riders were a lot closer to it than Slocum and the others. Getting there in time would be almost out of the question. But not quite. There was a slim chance the downhill run would make up for the difference. And Curly was hoping the sight of another band of riders might be just enough to give the raiders second thoughts. He didn't really think so, but it was best to just go ahead and do your job. You could think about it later.

They were closing on the *barranca* when the raiders reached it. As the raiders reined in, the dust began to thin, and Slocum saw more than a dozen men. Apaches. Dressed in loose-fitting shirts, breechcloths and the distinctive, thigh-length moccasins, half of them charged off their mounts and ripped away at the *barranca* walls, ignoring the razor-sharp thorns as they hurled the dislodged branches aside.

It was over in two minutes. A twenty-foot hole, more than big enough for the mustangs to escape, had been torn out of the huge circle. Curly cursed as he reached for his Winchester. All three men were still barreling across the valley floor as the Apaches sprang back to their mounts.

Three rode into the *barranca*, while the others charged past it to meet Curly, Rick and Slocum.

The Apaches fired first. Slocum skidded to a halt and dragged his carbine from the boot as he leapt from the saddle. Dropping to one knee, he took aim on the lead Apache. The shot went wide and slammed into a horse behind the leader. The animal went down, spilling his rider, who quickly scrambled onto the back of the next horse.

Curly, too, dismounted and stood flat-footed, firing almost as fast as he could lever shells into the chamber. The Apaches roared past, doing more yelling than shooting, but Rick Hardee bolted. Instead of letting the tide sweep past him, he turned his horse and made a break.

Three Apaches peeled off the main band and broke in pursuit. The others wheeled in a wide circle, ignoring the two defenders and sweeping back toward the *barranca*. Already, the mustangs were surging toward the opening in the wall, prodded by shouts and gunshots from the three Indians inside the walls.

Curly shook his fist as the first mustangs burst through the hole, then yanked his Colt revolver from his holster. At that range, even a lucky hit was unlikely, but Curly emptied the pistol in his frustration, hitting one of the mustangs. The animal fell, struggled to rise as the remainder of the herd surged past on either side, and was still on its knees as the three Apaches rode past.

One of the bucks slowed long enough to put the mustang out of its misery with a single shot from a revolver, then raced after the others.

Slocum sprang back into his saddle and broke after Hardee and the three warriors on his tail. Rick was almost to the foot of the rise, cutting at a sharp angle across the base of the slope. The Apaches were closing on him as his mount started up the slope. Slocum's roan was bigger than the Apache mounts, but they had a huge lead on him. He dug his spurs in, trying to wring the last ounce of speed from the big stallion. Rick fired once over his shoulder, then again, but the Apaches never slowed.

Slocum was still three hundred yards behind when Hardee's mount stumbled. It missed a step, then a second, and went down hard. Slocum saw Rick roll to one side as his horse fell over and rolled once, narrowly missing the frightened kid before scrambling to its feet.

The Apaches reined in as Rick threw his hands in the air and started to back up the hill. The Indians were fifty, maybe sixty feet away, laughing and pointing at Hardee. The kid turned and started to run.

Slocum fired once, but there was no way he could be accurate from horseback at that range. He saw the slug plow into the bone-dry dirt up the slope, sending a little puff of beige dust into the air.

One of the Apaches fired once, then again. Two more puffs of dust rose, neither more than a foot behind Hardee's desperate heels. It looked as if they weren't trying to hit him, as if scaring him were more fun. The kid was halfway up the hillside when one of the bucks spurred his mount and charged uphill after him.

Slocum fired again, this one coming close enough to get the Apaches' attention. The brave pursuing Hardee never looked back, but the other two wheeled their ponies and leveled their guns in Slocum's direction. They fired simultaneously. One bullet whistled past his ear as he ducked, and he saw the other shatter a small rock just a few feet in front of his horse.

He fired again, and the two bucks returned one more shot apiece before turning and starting up the slope after Hardee and their comrade.

Rick was on the ridgeline now, outlined against the brilliant, cloudless blue-white of the sky. He looked like a stick figure, his gangling limbs working spastically as he tried to run faster than was humanly possible. The lead Apache was closing fast now, pushing his pony. He leveled his Winchester as he rode past, and Slocum heard the crack of the rifle as Hardee fell backward, his arms clutching at his chest.

The kid sat up, braced with one arm, and went for his revolver then, but it was too late. The Apache fired again. The impact slammed the kid over on his back, and the Apache continued on over the ridge and down out of sight. The other two fired once more, again over their shoulders, and then they too were out of sight.

Slocum pushed on up the ridge, but he was no longer bent on pursuing the Apaches. Hardee might still be alive, although it seemed unlikely, and he had to make sure.

Dismounting a few yards below the crest of the ridge, Slocum sprinted the rest of the way and dropped to his knees alongside the splayed limbs of Rick Hardee. He was still breathing, but his chest was already a bright red smear, and Slocum could hear the gurgle of blood and air as Rick tried to breathe. His lungs weren't working properly, and Slocum pressed a palm flat and hard against the kid's chest.

The gurgling stopped, but Rick coughed once, then a second time, bursting large red bubbles between his lips. Slocum could see himself bent out of shape on the shiny surfaces before they burst. Then the bubbles stopped.

And Rick Hardee stopped breathing.

2

Slocum looked up as Curly dismounted. The foreman looked ashen. His hands were trembling as he knelt beside Hardee's corpse. "Sonofabitches," he said. "Bastards! They didn't have to do that. They already had the goddamn horses. What'd they have to do that for?" He reached out to brush a lock of hair off Hardee's forehead.

Turning to Slocum, he said, "Nineteen years old. That's all he was. What kind of life is that? Nineteen . . . Jesus Christ, Slocum, they didn't have to kill him."

Slocum nodded. Curly was right. But not for this time and this place. New Mexico was a land of hard rock and harder men. Even the plants were tougher than they had to be, armored with thick bark and thick-skinned leaves, armed with thorns two inches long and sharper than needles. The Indians who called it home had to be just as tough and just as ruthless. That's what it meant to survive here. The white men who followed them, then chased them out, pushing them into enclaves in the arid mountains, even chasing them across the border into Mexico, were no less hard. Curly knew that, and in a more serene moment, he would admit it.

But there was no room for serenity at the moment. Rick Hardee was dead. Nineteen or no, he had drawn his last breath. And there was only one thing on Curly's mind—

revenge. He stood up and looked back down at the *barranca,* now a broken circle, capable of holding nothing in, and it looked more than empty with the mustangs gone. It looked useless, as useless as Rick Hardee's death.

"Jesus, Slocum, what are we going to do? I got to tell Vern. The kid was his nephew, for Christ's sake. How am I going to tell him about this?" He looked at Rick's dead body, then at Slocum, then turned his back on both.

Slocum, still kneeling by the corpse, said, "You got to, Curly. I can't tell him. He wouldn't want to hear it from me."

"You don't know Vern, Slocum, not the way I do. He won't want to hear it at all. Not from you, not from me, not from nobody."

"I know, Curly, I know. But you have to tell him. You have to take Rick's body back for a decent burial."

"What the hell are you going to do?"

"Track them. If we're going to get those mustangs back, and get the men responsible for this, we have to know where they are. We give them enough time, they'll fall right off the earth. But the shooters will lead me to the others."

"You can't do that, Slocum."

"I have to, Curly. I'm not going to challenge them. I'll just track them, and I'll mark my trail. You get Vern and as many men as he can pull together and follow me. As long as I hang back, I'll be all right."

"Jesus, Slocum, you're crazy. You're a crazy man, that's the plain truth. You know that?"

"Maybe, but it's the only way. I go back with you, we lose them completely. You track them and I have to tell Vern. You know as well as I do that it can't be done like that."

Curly nodded. "I know it, 'course I do. I know it, but . . ." He knelt by the body again, across from Slocum. His hands were still shaking as he reached out with a thumb and pressed the eyelids closed. He drew back as if he'd been burned, then wiped his hand on his chaps. "I seen dead men before, Slocum. But not like this. I mean . . . "

"I know, Curly. I know. Give me a hand, will you? I got to get him up on his horse." Without waiting for an answer, he strode down the hill fifty yards or so to where Hardee's horse shook its head in between tugs at the bunchgrass. He glanced up as Curly approached, backed off a couple of steps, then stood as still as if he'd been cast in bronze.

Curly took the reins in one clenched fist and jerked them harder than necessary, as if he somehow blamed the horse for what had happened. The animal shook its head, trying to shake off the angry foreman, but surrendered as soon as it became clear that Curly was not going to let go.

Curly tugged the reluctant horse up the hill. He looked at Slocum for a long moment, then shook his head. "I guess we might as well do it," he said.

Still holding onto the reins, he knelt again, and together he and Slocum hoisted Hardee's limp body onto the saddle. Curly tied hands and feet together with a length of rawhide, then handed the reins to Slocum. Mounting his own horse, he nudged it close enough to lean over and take the reins of Hardee's mount.

"I sure as hell hope you know what you're doing, Slocum."

"Me too."

"Be careful." He tossed a stiff salute then turned away. Slocum watched Curly make his way down the hill, Hardee's mount drifting a little as it tagged along behind, its reins looped over Curly's saddle horn.

Slocum took off his hat and ran stiff fingers through his sweaty hair. He mopped his brow with a damp kerchief that smelled of salt, shoved it into his pocket, and slapped his hat back on. He swung up into the saddle, settled himself and gave the roan a spur. He wasn't sure what he was going to do, but he knew he had better watch his back. He wished he had an extra pair of eyes, and he sure as hell wished he had company. Since he had neither, he was determined to be as cautious as he knew how.

As long as he could stay reasonably close, they'd know where the Apaches had taken the horses. He could leave a clear trail, and Curly would be able to lead Vernon Settle and his hands with no difficulty.

There was one problem, and there was nothing he could do about it. The Apaches were notoriously cautious. Outnumbered as they were, and used to harassment by everyone from Comanches to Zunis, they had a habit of doubling back on their pursuers. They could probably trail him anyway, but since he was going out of his way to mark his route, a sweep would certainly pick him up. He had to hope the Apaches were more interested in putting some distance between themselves and the scene of the murder.

Driving nearly two hundred mustangs, they were not going to make great time. That meant the most direct route was the most likely. They didn't need that many horses, which meant they had probably been stolen for sale. But Settle had already had the horses branded. The only market was Mexico. And that was two hundred and fifty miles away.

Rather than follow the main band, Slocum elected to follow the three bucks who had murdered Rick Hardee. He couldn't afford to ignore them, and if anyone were going to ride the security sweep, it was those three. More than likely, they would fall in behind, partly to provide warning of any pursuit, and partly to deflect it. They knew that killing a white man in New Mexico was more likely to cause trouble than stealing a couple hundred horses.

The three bucks had not been worried about being followed when they broke over the ridge after shooting Hardee. That wouldn't last long, and Slocum pushed his mount to get on the trail as quickly as possible. He couldn't afford to stay within visual range, at least not with the naked eye. But for the glasses to do him any good, he'd have to have at least some idea of where his quarry had gone.

The broad, arid valley stretched out ahead of him, shallow as a meat platter. The dry ground didn't pick up prints easily, and the small Apache ponies were unshod, making it tougher still to pick up their tracks. But Slocum was used to it. He found a few scuff marks here and there—not much, maybe not even enough to catch the casual eye, but Slocum was anything but casual now. His life might depend on his vigilance.

An hour and a half later, he found a few horse apples. They were fresh. Even without getting down, he could tell that, maybe an hour old, if that. So, he knew the Apaches were still running, and he knew they'd widened the gap. But he still had them within range.

Shielding his eyes, he swept the end of the valley, more than two miles ahead. He didn't expect to see anything, but he didn't want to ride right up the barrel of an Apache Winchester, either. There was little cover available until the valley pinched closed and funneled through a notch between two slablike mesas.

He slowed his mount to a walk for a few minutes, squinting at the notch and trying to decide whether to go through or waste time and circle around one of the massive, blocky mesas. If he guessed right, he could save time, but if he guessed wrong, he'd lose even more than he stood to save if he won the gamble.

So he bit his lower lip and headed for the notch. The Apaches favored the high ground, and if they were laying for him, there was no better place. He let the roan choose its own pace, and twenty minutes later, he was close enough to throw a rock and hit the taller mesa, on the right. The canyon between them was only a hundred yards wide. Even smack down the center, he was within an easy rifle shot from either side.

The canyon floor was littered with gigantic slabs of reddish stone, great flakes that had peeled off the mesa walls and fallen like books from a shelf. Some had shattered and some lay in single pieces, as if some gigantic graveyard had been leveled by an indifferent hand no less gigantic.

Even the floor of the canyon wasn't safe. There was so much rubble heaped along the foot of either mesa, a hundred men could have hidden in the nooks and chinks, and it would take a thousand to smoke them out, even more if they were really determined to stay put.

Slocum was banking on flight as the most logical course of action for the three bucks. He hadn't seen any real sign for nearly a mile, maybe twice that, but it didn't take a strategist of genius to figure men on the move would have chosen the most direct route.

To be on the safe side, Slocum slipped from the saddle, hauled his carbine from its boot, and hugged the left-hand wall, pulling the roan beside him, using the horse to afford him some cover on the right-hand side. He'd hate to lose the horse, but there was no way, short of leaving it behind, to prevent anything from happening to it, so he figured he might as well protect himself as best he could.

He stopped every fifteen or twenty yards, straining his ears for some sign, but the canyon was dead quiet. Once, two hundred yards in, he heard a sharp crack. He hit the ground without thinking, wrenching his shoulder as the reins tangled in his right fist brought him up sharply. As he hit the ground, he heard a horrendous tearing sound, as if a huge piece of cloth were being ripped in two. Only then did he realize the crack hadn't been a gunshot.

He looked toward the sound, still gaining force, in time to see another broad, flat slab of stone finally tear free and tumble once as it pulled away from the wall, then plummet straight down two hundred feet before it landed on end just fifty yards away, hitting with enough force to make the ground tremble. The thunderous impact echoed twice then faded, and was replaced by the titter of hundreds of small fragments cascading down into the canyon and shattering into tinier pieces before skittering like stone beetles into the dust.

A plume of dust kicked up by the rockfall slowly flattened out, filling the sky above him with a fine, powdery cloud. It was already beginning to settle as he climbed to his feet and dusted himself off. It sifted down over everything, and the sky quickly regained its brilliant blue-white color.

His nerves were on edge, and he started to look back over his shoulder, wondering where in hell Curly and Settle were. He knew it was too soon for them to have caught up, but he felt more vulnerable than he was used to.

Something slammed into the dirt at his feet and he looked up at the canyon rim. The crack came a split second later, but it took him a few seconds to realize that this time it was a rifle shot. Belatedly, he hit the deck a second time.

He wasn't alone, had never believed he was, and hated knowing he had been right all along.

The question now was whether all three Apaches were somewhere above him or if only one had stayed behind to wage a delaying war. But neither answer was calculated to offer him much comfort. One Apache was all it took.

Just like it took only a single bullet.

3

Slocum scrambled into the rocks, letting his horse fend for itself. The roan was frightened, kept rearing up and shaking its head. Crawling under an overhanging slab of red stone, trying to push the thought of an angry rattler out of his head, he watched as the horse bolted back toward the mouth of the canyon.

Another shot cracked from somewhere high above him. The bullet glanced off the slab of rock and buried itself in the dry ground not six inches from his clenched fist. His boots butted up against the mesa wall, and he could go no further.

The cover was almost useless now, since they knew where he was, and he hadn't a clue where the Apaches might be, or even how many of them there were. But with ten tons of brittle stone cantilevered over his head, he felt a little less vulnerable and, for the moment, that was more than good enough. He had to think, to figure what his options were.

It didn't take long. He only had two. He could stay where he was, and defend his cramped niche like a lizard with bared fangs, or he could crawl back out, expose his spine to fire from the walls above and hope to God he could find someplace better. Hiding like a rat made him angry, but he was too smart to give in to it.

The numbers were the problem. If there was just one Apache, it was a Mexican standoff. To get a clear shot, the buck would have to expose himself to Slocum's Winchester. And Slocum could no more leave than the Indian could enter the shallow crevice. But if there were more than one, even as few as two, they had him by the short and curlies. Pincer him or wait him out, it was all the same. They could set up on either side of the opening, and wait for him to make a mistake. Like moving.

If they were tired of waiting around, they could smoke him out. It wouldn't take much to pile a mound of mesquite in front of the hole, and even less to get it blazing. Then he'd have Hobson's choice to make—he could die of smoke inhalation or a bullet. Either way, his eyes would be as glazed as Rick Hardee's, his heart as motionless in his dead chest. Some choice.

He listened intently for what seemed like a month. His pocket watch told him it was twenty minutes. But what was time to him now? He could hear nothing but the occasional click of a small rock dropping from the mesa walls and glancing off the boulders below. The sharp crack would echo once or twice, so faintly, like a tiny handclap far away. Then it would get quiet. Again.

Every time it happened, he imagined the moccasined foot that gave the rock its final impetus, and he waited to see the soft leather with its upcurved toe suddenly materialize at the edge of his hole. But it didn't happen. Not even when a rock glanced off the slab of stone above him and landed just beyond his reach in the dry, tan soil, kicking up a little puff of dust that drifted away like an impossibly small cloud or a short gasp on a winter afternoon.

He reached a point, after thirty minutes, when anything was preferable to lying there under a stone big enough to bury him and his entire family, sucking at the suffocating air and watching the slow shift of shadows as the sun drifted across the blue-white sky.

He made his decision, or realized that there really wasn't one to make—it was all the same. Stretching his legs, pushing his bootheels against the stone behind him, he

slid toward the bright patch of sunlight. He could hear the
scrape of his shirt buttons on the dry ground, the gouging
of his belt buckle as it plowed a shallow furrow in the earth,
and he could hear the rattle of his own breath in his parched
throat. He wanted a drink of water, but his canteen was out
of reach.

Slowly, he pushed himself until his fingers rested on
the sharply etched line between light and shadow. Clearly,
Slocum could see one fingernail gleaming in the sunlight,
the thin band of shade outlining the fingertip on the bright
soil. He watched the hand for a moment, almost detached,
like a man watches an insect settle on a quiet stream. He
knows there's a trout, he just doesn't know whether the trout
knows, or cares, about the insect. The uncertainty made his
heart beat faster, his breath grow shallow and rapid.

And nothing happened.

The waiting was killing him. For all he knew, the Apaches
were long gone. Better to find out the quick way, even if it
was the hard way. The slab of stone wouldn't permit him to
get up on his knees, so his start would be slow. Once in the
clear, he could change directions and maybe get a fix. If the
Apaches didn't get him first. Crawling like a crab, he moved
into the sunlight. He felt his back muscles grow taut as he
waited for the impact of a bullet. The thought pushed him
faster and he scrambled all the way into the clear, raising
himself up too soon and ripping his back against the jagged
underside of the stone. But he was out and moving.

Springing to his feet, he sprinted across the canyon, waiting for the next shot. When it came, he was almost happy.
The bullet sailed harmlessly past, and he heard it glance off
the stone and slam into the sun-baked ground. Another shot
cracked, its echo joining that of the first, and dying away a
little more quickly.

As near as he could tell, both were from the same position, but he couldn't stop to look. Running a jagged line,
he turned as sharply as he could without slowing down,
and dove into a cluster of large rocks near the center of the

canyon. He had some cover now, but more importantly, he
had a decent view of most of the mesa walls on either side.
A broken chimney of stone, two large layered hunks of it
lying on their sides beside it, gave him plenty of protection from the right-hand wall. The stones on the left were
smaller, but still gave him enough cover to let him lie on
his belly and scan the lip of the canyon two hundred feet
above.

The canyon was silent again. He still wore the glasses
around his neck and put them to good use. Starting with
the lip of the mesa on the left, he tracked it from the mouth
of the canyon all the way out of rifle range ahead. Rolling
onto his back and propping himself against a small, roundish
boulder, he checked the opposite rim. Both, as near as he
could tell, were clear.

The Apaches, if they were still there, were somewhere
lower down. The mesa walls were uneven, studded with
flutes and chimneys of red stone. He could see winding
trails, most floored with loose sand, snake through the rocks
in every direction, some up and then down, some ending in
blind alleys. It was a maze, and he was not about to get lost
in it. Better, he thought, to wait. Let them come to him. If
they were still there.

He wriggled in between two larger rocks and swept the
face of the right-hand mesa, working patiently with the
glasses. He knew the chances of spotting anyone were slim.
The Indians had binoculars of their own, almost certainly,
and since they knew where he was, they could conceal
themselves until he looked elsewhere, then change posi-
tions, working their way through the maze in fits and starts,
moving only through ground he had already covered.

By the time he'd completed his survey, he knew it was
pointless. But there was nothing else he could do, short of
exposing himself a second time and rushing into the maze
where he'd lose every edge he had, and there were only two
as it was—he was pretty well concealed now, and it was not
possible to get close to him without the risk of exposure.

Once he left the relative security of the boulders, he'd play into their hands.

He had heard enough stories from old-timers about the Apaches. They could move without a sound, and they knew most of the land between Colorado and the Sierra Madres better than most white men knew their own counties.

Curly had told him how the Apaches trained their children, taking them into the mountains under the tutelage of a warrior, letting them learn from those who knew best, cutting them loose for days at a time. The children, both boys and girls, would have to fend for themselves. The teacher was always within range to help, but the children didn't know that. They sank or swam on their own, as far as they knew.

It made them good and it made them tough. They spent their lives in the rocky wasteland, managing to thrive where others had to struggle just to hang on by their fingernails. These were not the kind of men Slocum was anxious to confront on alien ground.

Sweeping the rocky faces at random, now, he hoped for a break. He'd whip the binoculars from place to place, trying to keep them off balance. If he got lucky, maybe he'd catch sight of a red headband, maybe the shadow of an arm moved just a fraction too late. Hell, if there was a God in heaven, he thought, he might even pick up the flash of sunlight on a lens or a rifle barrel. But it had been a long time since he knew, or cared, whether there was a heaven itself, let alone whether it was occupied and by whom.

Getting to his knees, Slocum peered up toward the rim again, this time with the naked eye. He wanted, needed, some movement, something to tip the scales a little in his favor. Raising the Winchester, he sighted along the barrel. The scarred wooden stock felt warm in his hands, the metal, polished so often it no longer glittered, felt warmer still. The heavy carbine swept almost mechanically along the rimrock, his eye wide, tracing the dark line of stone against the superheated sky.

And he got his break. Something moved, darker than the sky, but not so dark as the rock. Not wanting to let on that he had seen something, he continued to move the gun, but kept his eye focused on the movement. It wasn't much, but he wasn't wrong. It moved again, whatever it was. A sleeve, tan, but not quite as tan as the stone on which it rested.

Dropping back on his haunches, he leaned against a boulder, still moving the gun barrel as if he were continuing to trace the rimrock behind the bead of the lead sight. Then, feigning disgust, he let it waver, then fall. His jaw ached with the tension as he reached for the glasses again, started at the mouth of the canyon and worked his way back.

And there it was. An arm, curled around the stone. He could see the individual fingers, hugging the rock, resting on a slight outcropping of the massive boulder. He twiddled the focus to sharpen the image. The hand dropped away, but he had a target now.

Wriggling in among the boulders, Slocum curled around the base of the rock chimney. He brought the Winchester forward and let it rest on a jagged boulder edge. He waited, squinting, for the hand to reappear or, better still, a shoulder, something he could shoot at with a chance of hitting it.

The Apache was patient. Slocum had to give him at least that. The seconds ticked by, turned into minutes. Somewhere a stone fell, shattered on stone and sent its pieces skittering like locusts down into the dry soil. Slocum listened, then wondered whether he was being decoyed. Could the hand have been placed there on purpose, to catch his attention and hold it? he wondered. Were they *that* subtle?

On a hunch, he squirmed part way around in the narrow cranny in which his body lay like a casket in a grave, flush against both sides of a depression large enough to hold it and not much larger. He checked the opposing rim. He almost screamed as he saw the second Indian, erect now, a rifle just coming to rest on a rock ledge. A hundred and thirty feet up and fifty yards down the canyon, the Apache waited patiently for Slocum to give him a clear shot.

He waited a second too long.

Slocum brought his Winchester up slowly, not wanting to alert the marksman that he had been seen. Rolling on one hip, feeling the sharp edges of the stone scrape at his back and knees, he sighted slowly, almost casually. He saw the headband, the bead of his sight resting dead center on the red cloth, then raised it an inch, then two.

The bullet would drop a little, and Slocum wanted to make a point. He wanted to make sure. Chewing at his lower lip, he tightened his finger on the trigger, held his breath . . . and squeezed. The gun bucked, the butt slammed into his shoulder, and he lowered it in time to see the Apache's rifle begin to spiral as it arced out and away from the wall. The Indian slammed back against the rock wall, seemed to bounce off it, then pitched forward.

The sound of the gunshot banged again and again off one wall then the other, back and forth, back and forth, slowly finding its way up and out of the canyon. The Indian fell head downward. On the back of his shirt, there was a red stain clearly visible in the brilliant sunshine, then he plunged into shade and Slocum lost sight of him for a second.

He heard the dull thud of the body landing, not loud enough to echo. And it was silent again.

4

"That's one," Slocum mumbled. Quickly, he jerked the rifle back around, looking for the second Apache. There was no sign of the Indian high on the rim. But he still couldn't risk the open, because if there were two, there was almost certainly a third. The three Apaches who had killed Rick Hardee were without doubt sticking together.

Another shot rang out, and Slocum ducked instinctively, knowing that the bullet would already have hit him if it were going to. He heard an inhuman shriek, and it didn't register at first. Then, when he heard his horse nicker, he looked back through the rocks to where the roan had been and saw the animal lying on its side. The bullet had found its mark after all.

The Apaches were planning to make a break. Killing Slocum's horse would leave him unable to follow. He shook a fist at the rim, but the Indians didn't even pay him the respect of another shot. Ammunition was hard to come by for the Apaches, and they were known to pass up even easy targets if there was nothing to be gained. Which made it all the more curious for them to have taken the time and trouble to shoot Hardee.

Slocum didn't understand it then, and he didn't understand it now . . . unless they were covering something up. He pushed the thought aside and reached for the glasses again. A cursory sweep of the rock face yielded nothing. He hadn't expected it to, and he knew instinctively that he could walk to his horse straight up without fear. The Apaches were gone.

Still, he couldn't afford to take the chance. He waited and watched. Twenty minutes went by, then forty. There hadn't been another sound since the gunshot that felled his mount. After an hour, he stood, cautiously but resolutely. Slowly, he exposed himself to the rimrock until he was standing erect.

Nothing.

Shaking his head, he walked slowly toward the roan, still lying on its side and snuffling. A pool of blood spread out from its side. It had soaked into the dry ground, and glistened with a greenish glaze. The animal was all but dead now, and he did the only decent thing. The gunshot report slapped at him off the walls, slowly died away, and the horse lay still at last.

Slocum knelt to retrieve his canteen and saddlebags, loosened the cinch and jerked the saddle free, bracing himself with both feet against the roan's backbone to tug the cinch out from under the lifeless horse. He wasn't going to lug the saddle, but he didn't want it to lie there, either. It wouldn't take long for the already rotting corpse to draw more than its share of buzzards and coyotes. He watched a fly land on the roan's open eye, still half-expecting the animal to blink. When he allowed himself to admit it wouldn't happen, he carried the saddle fifty feet to a small pocket among some small boulders, and concealed it.

He walked back to the dead horse, retrieved his saddlebags and canteen from the ground, looped them over his left shoulder, and started walking. No way in hell he was going to try to follow the Apaches on foot. There was only one way to go, and that was back out through the mouth of the canyon.

With any luck, he wouldn't have to walk that far. Settle, Curly and some of the hands should already be close by.

He'd left a clear trail for them to follow. Now, all he had to do was backtrack until they picked him up. He heard the first flutter of great wings when he was no more than thirty yards away. He glanced back, saw the wings fold as the buzzard landed near the dead horse, then he turned away. He'd seen it before.

The sun pressed down on him like a white-hot hand. It was high in the sky and behind him as he trudged northeast. He could feel the trickle of sweat down his spine, and he watched his demoralized shadow retreat ahead of every step. Even the ground was too bright to stare at for too long, and he squinted away the glare, closing his eyes every so often to give them a little relief.

As he passed out of the canyon, he looked back one more time. Standing there with the saddlebags over his shoulder, he couldn't help but feel as if he had been defeated in some way he didn't understand. He felt impossibly small as he looked up at the towering walls of the canyon, standing there with boulders twice his height scattered around like so many insignificant pebbles on the bank of a creek. It was a feeling he didn't like, and one he was determined to reverse.

He wanted to get even. That was only natural. But the more he thought about the cold-blooded killing of Rick Hardee, the more he thought there must be something to it that he didn't know, something that would change his perspective. But one thing didn't change, and that was that two of the men responsible were still alive. And that, too, would have to change.

Turning his back on the canyon, he trudged away from the sun, occasionally shielding his eyes with one palm and staring off across the flat, barren wasteland. Everything around him was twisted, stunted, unnatural seeming. The bright glare washed out most of the color. Even the plants looked like blackened hulks, as if some great conflagration had ripped across the land and left nothing but ashes behind.

After an hour, the sun started to go down, and a slight

breeze rippled clouds of dust across his field of vision. His water was running low, and he shifted his course to head for a stand of junipers off to the north. There would be a water hole, but it was still three or four miles away. He'd be lucky to reach it by sundown.

The light changed imperceptibly, bathing everything with an orange wash as the sun slipped further down. Already, the mesas far behind him had lost their reddish color. Their tops were purple, and lower down they were dark gray. The ground underfoot was getting rockier, and he was climbing uphill now, not steeply, but enough that the steady rise had begun to take its toll. Slocum downed the last of his water when he was still a mile from the junipers.

He worried that he might have miscalculated. There was still no sign of Curly or Settle, and in half an hour, it would be too dark to see more a few feet, at least until moonrise. Almost unconsciously, he checked his pocket for matches, found a dozen or so in a small box, and turned his attention to the small oasis.

If he could gather enough dead wood, he could build a fire bright enough to attract attention. It was a risk, because the Apaches just might be curious about it, but it would be worse to miss Curly. Even with water, there was no way he could make it back to the spread in less than three days. Assuming he *could* make it, the Apaches and the mustangs would be long gone. Pushing the stolen horses hard, they would make the Mexican border in four days, maybe five at the outside.

Once they crossed into Mexican territory, they would sell the horses and disappear into the Sierra Madres. They had been doing that for centuries, and they owned the mountains. The Mexican army had lost hundreds of men in futile attempts to penetrate the mountains, while the Apaches had lost only a relative handful. Even the U.S. Cavalry had had little success, and that precious little had depended more on luck and the work of Apache scouts than any particular military competence.

No, if Vernon Settle was going to get his mustangs back, he'd have to do it in the next four days.

The sun bloodied itself on the jagged edge of the Chiricahua Mountains to the west, then slowly sank out of sight just as Slocum stumbled into the knee-deep grass leading up to the junipers and the water hole beyond them. He knelt by the small pool, swept the green glaze aside and buried his face in the tepid water. He rinsed his mouth, swirling the water to soothe his parched lips and tongue. The water tasted stale, but it was drinkable.

The first mouthful went down hard, his dry throat resistant to the sudden rush of liquid. The second was easier, and he deferred a third, unwilling to endure the cramps he knew would follow too much too soon.

He lay back and took a deep breath. The thick fragrance of the grass crushed beneath him seemed alien to him, and he inhaled again, this time noticing the pungent scent of the junipers, too. He got to his feet and snatched at a few dead branches, mostly small, some still bearing the pulpy needles of the juniper. Closer to the water, a dead cottonwood leaned over, its roots exposed above a great gouge in the earth where it had fallen.

Working more quickly, he snapped several of the smaller branches, arranged them in a heap and scraped a bare patch in the ground to make room for his fire. The bone-dry tinder caught almost at once, and he tossed some of the thicker kindling on, then teepeed some of the thickest branches.

The wood was so dry, it was going to burn quickly, and he was too tired even to consider the prospect of staying up all night to feed the flames. Hacking at the dead cottonwood with his boot knife, he got enough fuel to last an hour or so, then sat down to consider how to handle his dilemma.

If he fell asleep and the fire went out, he'd miss Curly. If he stayed awake, he'd be exhausted in the morning and be forced to cover less ground. Either way, he was the loser. But without an ax, those were his only choices.

Back at the cottonwood, he put his back into an attempt

to snap some of the thicker branches, and one broke off suddenly. Still attached by a thin strip of bark, it had to be twisted before he could drag it to the fire. Snapping the smaller branches off, he propped the thick branch at a steep angle against some rocks, hoping the sheer weight of the wood would keep feeding the blaze, but knowing, too, that the flames would climb up the branch and burn it far faster than he wanted.

In the uncertain light, he searched the oasis for more fuel, but except for a couple of stunted brown junipers, he found nothing small enough to move that was dry enough to burn. It was up to whatever luck he hadn't already used to get him through this one.

Slocum was hungry, and he searched for some strips of dried beef in his saddlebags. He had four, and allowed himself only one, uncertain when he would be able to fill his stomach again. The meat was salty and made him thirsty all over again. He uncapped his canteen for another drink, capped it and tossed it aside. He leaned back to close his eyes for a moment.

In the back of his mind was a gnawing doubt. Rick Hardee's face kept fading in and out of focus. Somehow, he was convinced that Hardee was not killed by chance. He had run, true, but that should not have been enough to get him killed. Somehow, he was suddenly convinced, Hardee had been connected to the raid. Maybe he had told the Apaches about the *barranca,* maybe he had told someone who told them. But there was method in the murder, and Rick Hardee had been killed to shut him up.

But he couldn't take it any further than that. It would never get anyone indicted, let alone convicted, but he was convinced there was more to this than met the eye.

Slocum heard something, a sound off in the distance, meaningless maybe, but indisputably there. He strained his ears, but the noise was gone. With the sun down, it was getting chilly, and he moved closer to the fire for a few moments to take the chill off. But the crackling flames would drown out any repeat of the sound, so he backed away again, moving out to the very edge of the imperfect circle of light cast by the fire.

Listening intently, he moved through the grass and stood on the edge of the green. The junipers were behind him. He could hear the breeze sift through the branches, and that, too, was too loud. Moving still further into the darkness, he looked up at the sky. Judging by the stars, it would be a while before moonrise.

Then he heard it again, possibly a horse, he thought. Instinctively, he moved toward the sound. He looked back at the fire. Its flames were still flickering brightly. It should be possible on this level ground to see it for a mile or more. He was less than half that off the trail he'd left, but it seemed impossible to believe that Curly or Settle could follow even so plain a trail in the darkness.

Unless they'd guessed where the Apaches had headed. But how could they have known?

And that brought him back to Rick Hardee.

Again.

5

"Slocum . . . ? You there?" It was Curly. Slocum had nearly jumped out of his skin. The massed shadows between him and the fire had dismounted now, and as the men gathered closer to the flames, he could see Vernon Settle, his stone face impassive under the tumble of white whiskers, more biblical than human.

Heaving a sigh, he lowered the hammer on the Winchester and stepped out of the junipers. "Over here, Curly."

Haines spun in his tracks and shook his head. "Christ, I thought maybe you was dead. You damn fool, you never should have gone after them Apaches on your own."

Settle stepped in front of Curly and pushed his hat back off his head. It hung by a beaded string, draped over his shoulders. His mass of white hair was smashed flat by the Stetson, and he looked as if he hadn't slept in a week. "You all right, boy?" he asked.

Slocum nodded, then took the extended hand. It felt like scarred oak in his palm, and the old man leaned forward to peer at him. "My eyes ain't what they used to be, boy," he said. "Come over by the fire and let me get a look at you." Without waiting for an answer, Settle turned and walked toward the fire.

Slocum, not knowing what else to do, followed him. Settle dropped to his haunches and grabbed a branch sticking

29

out of the flames. He stirred the fire and sent a column of sparks high into the air. The fire brightened, and Settle let the stick go. "What happened out there, Slocum?"

Curly said, "I already told you, Vern."

"I want to hear it from somebody else now, Curly. You shut up and let Slocum talk." He scowled over his shoulder at Haines for a moment, then looked back at Slocum. "Go on, son, tell me what you saw."

Slocum told him. The old man listened without comment. When Slocum stopped talking, and the silence grew long enough for Settle to know there was no more to come, he asked, "And what do you think about it?"

"What's to think?" Slocum answered. "Apaches ran off the horses. It wasn't the first time."

"It'll by God be the last. For them bucks, anyhow. I'll see to that. But I want to know what you *really* think."

Slocum hesitated, and the old man leaned a little closer. He sensed something, and he was determined to shake it loose. "Anything seem funny to you?"

"No, not really."

"Nothing just a little out of plumb with all this?"

"No sir, Mr. Settle, I . . ."

"Don't hold back, boy. Somethin's bothering you. I can smell it. Tell me what it is."

"Well, I was wondering why they chased Rick down. They didn't have to kill him. Hell, he was running the other way. No need. It was pointless."

"Was it?"

"Seems like."

Settle nodded. He reached back and grabbed Haines by the pant leg. "Git over here, Curly. Set down." He slapped the ground with a huge palm, then used the same hand to pull Curly down beside him. "What do you think about what Slocum here just said?"

Curly shrugged. "It was Apaches, Vernon. When do they ever need an excuse for murder?"

"All right, let's say you're right. Yet and still, they got

what they come for. It ain't like them, especially lately, to go out of their way for trouble. You know that as well as I do, Curly. Why'd they kill that boy, then?"

"Because he was a white man and they're Indians. That's just the way it is."

"That simple, then?"

"That simple. How I see it, anyways."

Slocum started to take it a step further, but changed his mind. He was a new hand. Some of the others had known Rick Hardee all their lives. And he was Vernon Settle's nephew. There was no point in cutting himself off by casting suspicions on a dead man in front of his friends. And his uncle. Maybe he could get a word alone with Settle. That would be better. Settle noticed the indecision, and gave Slocum a searching look, but he didn't push.

The old man stood up. "Reckon we should turn in. Curly, you post a couple of guards. Have somebody relieve 'em in four hours. No sense in us forgetting where we are or what we're up against."

"Yes, sir, Mr. Settle." Curly moved off to make the arrangements, and Settle moved to his horse and got his bedroll. He came back near the fire and dropped the bedroll on the ground. Slocum hadn't moved, and Settle looked at him. "No bedroll, son?"

"Too much to carry."

Settle nodded. He nudged his own roll with the toe of one boot. "Use this one, then."

"Thanks, but that's all right. I don't need it."

"The hell you don't, Slocum. You took a damn-fool chance runnin' after them Apaches by yourself. Don't sacrifice any more than you have to. Understand? It doesn't pay. These men'll think you a fool, and there's nobody else that matters."

Slocum thanked the old man and straightened. He moved around the fire and snatched at the bedroll, then moved back away from the fire a bit and made up his bed. He lay the Winchester by his side and used the saddlebags for a pillow.

Taking off his gunbelt, he made a tight coil of the leather and set it beside the saddlebags. He lay down on the blanket and shifted his body to avoid the prod of a couple of sharp stones, then patted the butt of the Colt Navy to make certain it was within easy reach.

Rolling in, he closed his eyes and was asleep immediately.

It was still dark when Slocum awoke. The fire had dwindled, but one of the sentries must have been feeding it a few branches now and then because it was still crackling. Slocum sat up, and watched the moon, which had risen after he'd gone to sleep and now was almost ready to disappear again.

Something rustled in the junipers, then with a flap of wings an owl exploded out of the tallest of them and climbed in a tight spiral. Still tired, Slocum knew he was done sleeping for the night. He rolled out of the blanket and pulled his boots on, then buckled on his gunbelt.

He walked to the edge of the water hole and sat down with his back against a rock.

"Can't sleep, Slocum?"

He heard a rustle, and Vernon Settle materialized out of the shadows and lowered himself to the ground. He leaned back against the same rock. Slocum looked at the old man and for a moment thought he had been cast from pewter. The moonlight had silvered the leathery skin, and turned the white hair and beard to pale gray.

"What are you doing awake, Mr. Settle?"

The old man chuckled. "Hell, Slocum, was my horses them Apaches run off. I'm too damn mad to sleep. Besides, you get to be my age, you figure time's running out. No point wasting it with your eyes closed. Know what I mean?"

Slocum knew. He remembered his grandfather talking the same way, more years ago than he cared to remember. It seemed when a man got old, he went one of two ways. Either he suddenly got religion, and started making up for all the mistakes he'd made, hoping it wasn't too late to earn a little forgiveness, or he decided that he was never going to get the chance to make enough mistakes unless he worked real hard at it for the rest of his allotted time. Vernon Settle was one of the latter.

"You know, Slocum," Settle said, "all I got is my land, my horses and my little girl. It ain't much to leave behind. When I was a boy, I thought the world wasn't big enough for the man I was going to be. I needed two, three worlds. That's how much vinegar I had. But the older I got, the bigger the world got. Wasn't long before I realized just how dumb I was. And when Ginny was born, I felt like a speck, that's how small. You can't believe a thing like that until it actually happens, I guess. But you see that little bitty thing, squalling and kicking and it makes you wonder . . ."

"Seems to me you've done all right."

"Seems so, don't it? But I just don't know. Ginny's what matters. And I don't think I've done what I should've for her. Once her mother died, I . . . aww, what the hell, Slocum. You ain't interested in this. An old man's rambling. Boring shit, all of it. Self-indulgent, too. I guess all I mean is, you get a chance to make a life for yourself, make sure it's what you really want. I never done that, and I'm sorry as all hell."

"Virginia doesn't seem to have any complaints."

" 'Course not. She's too polite by half. But she's gonna make a fine woman in another year or two. Already is, I guess, but her old man don't want to let go just yet, let her be, let her live her own life."

Settle trailed off, and Slocum let the old man have his silence. There was more than a little pain there, and Slocum didn't know him half well enough to help. It was better to be still.

"You know," Settle said, "I sent for the Army over to Fort Stillwell. Don't know if it'll do any good, but . . ."

"They take their sweet time, usually."

"Too much rigamarole, Slocum. That's what it is. You in the war?"

Slocum nodded. Then, realizing the old man wasn't looking at him, he said, "Yeah, I was."

"Lucky to be here, then, ain't you?"

"I guess."

"Don't guess, Slocum. Believe it. Every damn minute you're alive, thank your stars. Suck all the juice out of it, by God, because you only get but one chance."

"You think the Army can help?" Slocum asked.

"Help? Hell, I don't know. Never did before. 'Course, there's something funny going on, Slocum. This ain't the first time I lost a bunch of horses. But by Godfrey, it'll be the last, if I have anything to say about it."

"The Apaches can't be far. We'll find them."

"Maybe so, Slocum, maybe so. But you got to hand it to them. It'll take more than a pocketful of ranch hands to bring them down. I don't even give a damn about the Indians, really. All I want is to get my horses back. I met Cochise once. Before the war. Quite a fellow. Had eyes could see your damn bones, he looked through you that easy. And it ain't all their fault, neither."

"What do you mean?"

"Ever ask yourself why the Apaches keep raising hell? Ever ask yourself where they get the guns and ammunition? Where they get the whiskey? Don't take a professor to figure it out. Somebody's making money, Slocum. And I would bet everything I own he's got a white skin."

"I wanted to ask you about Rick Hardee."

"What about him?"

"Why do you think they killed him?"

"I wish to hell I knew, Slocum. But I don't. You know anything, you better tell me."

"I don't know anything special. But I can't help but think they were after him particularly. Like they had some special reason."

"Like what?"

"I don't know. But . . ."

"You keep that to yourself, boy. But you just might be onto something. He was my sister's boy, but . . ." He waved a helpless hand, then let it flutter to his lap, where it continued to twitch like a broken-winged bird.

6

As the sun came up, Settle added some wood to the fire and put up coffee. Then he walked among the sleeping hands, prodding each with a booted toe, and cursing them good-naturedly. When he'd managed to rouse them all, he sat down to wait until they'd washed and poured themselves a cup of coffee. Rollie Larkin, the outfit's cook, was working on some biscuits and bacon, and Settle outlined his intentions for the day.

"You all know we sent somebody over to Fort Stillwell. What I suggested to Colonel Martin, and what we sure as hell got to hope he agreed with, was to send a detachment to meet us at Copper Canyon, on the Mimbres River. According to all my experience, and just about everything we know about the situation suggests this is typical, them Apaches are most likely gonna head for the border, crossing down into Mexico, and moving on down to the horse market at Ciudad Bolivar in Chihuahua. Them Mexicans have never been too particular where horses come from, and they pay *mucho dinero* for good stock. Most of you boys seen the mustangs they run off. They'll bring top dollar, and who-ever is leading them renegades'll know that. Chow down, and don't take it easy, because we won't eat again until we hook up with the Army boys. However long it takes."

With that, Settle walked out into the open ground around

the water hole and stared at the horizon. With the sun just above the edge of the world, the colors of the Florida Mountains were still deep reds and purples. It was an austere beauty, more awe inspiring than delightful, and it made Slocum more than a little melancholy to look at it.

The men whispered among themselves. There wasn't one of them who wasn't aware that at best they were outmanned nearly two to one. In open country, those odds wouldn't frighten most of them. The hands were better armed, more than likely, and almost certainly had more ammunition. But they were heading into the Florida range, and with every foot they climbed, the odds shifted more dramatically toward the Apaches. And once they headed down into the flatlands leading to the border, the Indians would know they were just about home free. It would become a race, plain and simple. And each man knew that if it came to that, the Apaches had already won.

In the back of Slocum's mind as they headed out was a single question. He knew the Army was already spread far too thin. If Settle and the others were expecting to be met by a large column, they were almost certain to be disappointed. During the night, Slocum had suggested as much, but Settle brushed it away. He claimed that he and Colonel Martin were well acquainted, and that Martin was just as anxious as every white man in New Mexico Territory to put the run to the Apaches.

With such good intentions, as Slocum well knew, a well-known road had been paved more than once. The men were quiet as they rode. There was none of the usual banter and the good-natured insults with which men on the move usually passed the time. The sky seemed to be squeezing the life out of them. They were more than quiet, Slocum thought. They were almost sullen.

Vernon Settle rode apart, not out of any sense of superiority, but rather because it was his nature. He was a man who was uncomfortable in large groups, regardless of the reason. He preferred his own company. He was too contemplative to mix easily with the men, and they seemed to adopt his demeanor almost by osmosis.

When they reached the cut where Slocum had lost his mount, Settle called a halt. Dropping from his mount, the old man said, "Listen up. Slocum, here, is gonna tell us what happened here. Go ahead, son."

"Nothing to tell, Mr. Settle. I followed the three bucks who killed Rick Hardee. When I got here, I slowed a bit, knowing how the Apaches like an ambush if they can arrange it. They got my horse and I got one of them."

"Fair trade, seems like to me," Settle said.

The men laughed brittlely, but the laughter died quickly, and Slocum said, "That's all there is to tell, really."

Settle nodded. "I like that. No histrionics. No bull. Plain and simple. That's the best way. You go on and get your gear. Make it quick. The rest of you, you got to pee, now's the time. You ain't done when Slocum's got his gear ready, you got to catch us up anyway you can."

Slocum dug his saddle out of the niche where he'd hidden it, then saddled and haltered one of the half-dozen fresh horses Settle had brought along. He selected another roan, a little younger, and a lot friskier than his five-year-old stallion had been. When he tightened the cinch and swung up into the saddle, he heard a loud shriek. Instinctively, he went for the Colt, but Settle said, "Hold up, it's just one of the boys. Look yonder."

Slocum spotted him almost at once. It was Bill LaBarge, a big blond kid who had been friendly with Rick Hardee. He was standing on a flat rock holding something high over his head. Slocum blinked away the bright sun, then blew up in disgust when he realized what it was. "Dammit, Bill. What the hell's wrong with you?"

"Butt out, Slocum. I got me a trophy, sure enough. Sumbitch killed Rick and I got his hair to hang on the goddamned wall when I get home."

"Apaches don't take scalps. Hell, you're worse than any Indian."

"Shut your mouth, Slocum," LaBarge said. "I done it, and I'm glad I done it, and you got nothin' to say about it."

Settle spoke up before Slocum could respond. "Slocum's right," he said. "No call to act like a savage, Billy."

"Hell, Vernon, I *am* a savage. Might as well act like one."

The men laughed, but Settle shook his head. "Won't tell you again, Billy. Put it back."

"Left my needle and thread to home, Mr. Settle. Right there in the bunkhouse, along with Slocum's balls."

Slocum made a move, but Settle reached out and grabbed his arm. He walked toward the rock and climbed up with the ease of a man half his age. "Won't tell you again, Billy. Put it back."

"Mr. Settle, I—"

"Now! I don't want to hear no guff, Billy. Now, God damn it! Git on your horse and let's move."

By noon, they had covered forty miles. They were making good time—better, even, than Slocum had imagined. The sun hammered at them, and the earth shimmered in the rising air currents. Even the mountains seemed to be melting. Slocum shielded his eyes, and it looked as if everything ahead, as far as he could see, was under thick, clear water.

He watched Vernon Settle closely. The old man seemed to be a bundle of contradictions. As angry as he was at the death of Rick Hardee and the loss of his horses, he still seemed almost benign in some ways, as if he understood the Apaches, or forgave them. The hands were less forgiving.

Falling back in the pack, he listened to them grumble. More than one thought Settle should have let Billy LaBarge have the scalp. Slocum found himself wondering if there was any difference. The Apaches did what they had to do, and the white men seemed to want to meet them on their own ground, trade one brutality for another. He understood human nature well enough to know that nobody could win that kind of contest. The War Between the States had proved that to anyone with half a brain. All you did was drag it on, make the other side try to outdo you, and force yourself to outdo them.

In the end, there were more dead than anyone could live with. And that, too, was plain for anyone to see.

At one-thirty, the sun off to the right now, slanting down into their eyes and forcing them to shove their hats far forward, Slocum spotted a small cloud to the west and slightly north. He called Settle's attention to it, and the old man called for a change of course. "Probably the Army," he said. He didn't sound particularly pleased, and Slocum found himself wondering exactly what the old man really wanted.

They were closing on the cloud at a good clip, and Slocum watched the dust hang in the air for a long time, trailing up on the heated air, then spreading in a long rooster tail until it gradually drifted away to a fine haze. It took nearly a half hour for the cavalry detachment to crystallize in the shimmering heat. It didn't look large, and Slocum eased his horse alongside Settle's big chestnut.

"Doesn't look like the Army sent much help," Slocum said.

Settle smiled with the lower half of his face, but his eyes remained cold and distant. "Didn't expect they would, Slocum. There's more to all this than meets the eye. I figured they'd put in an appearance, but not much more."

"How come?"

"I'll tell you some other time. Right now, I got to think about things a little."

"Whatever you say, Mr. Settle."

"Slocum, tell me something."

"What's that?"

"The rest of the boys all call me Vern or Vernon. Why don't you?"

"Not the way I was raised, Mr. Settle."

"I appreciate the manners, Slocum, but out here, they

ain't necessary. Just because I'm older and pay your wages, you don't have to think I'm any better'n you are."

"There's more to good manners than that, Mr. Settle."

"There's more to most things, son. But we're all in this together. Might as well act like it."

"Yes, sir." Slocum smiled. To his surprise, Settle returned it. And this time it didn't stop at the lower half of his face. It was the first genuine smile Slocum could remember from him.

"You think we ought to chase them Apaches all the way to Mexico, Slocum?"

"You would know that better than I would. I don't know much about them."

"Let me tell you something, then. You look around you. Look at the land. Hard. Then ask yourself what kind of man you have to be to try and live here. A man can do that, seems to me you have to respect him. You don't have to like him, but you sure as hell have to give him credit. That's the difference between me and most of the other ranchers around these parts. They think the Apaches are nothing but animals. I look at it like this: we don't own the land, the land owns us. That means we play by its rules if we want to stay alive. The Apaches know that, and they've managed. Until we got here, anyway . . ."

"That's not a widely held view, I imagine."

"Slocum, most of the half-wits around here don't realize we didn't have to fight the Apaches. A lot of them who do know it don't give a good goddamn. We done a lot to make it bad, and once it got bad, we done our damndest to make it worse yet. For my money, I'd as soon have Apaches as neighbors as half the men I know. But there are rules, and I got to play by 'em. I don't have to like it, and between me and you, I don't much, but there you have it."

"So you'd rather not fight them, is that it?"

"What I'd rather has nothing to do with anything, Slocum. We made a fair mess of things out here—the white men, I mean. But if you stand in the muck, you clean it up.

Standing there with your thumb in your ear and worryin' about how it came to be don't help none. The way things stand, any white man is fair game when one of them bucks takes a notion to go on the prowl. They took my animals. They killed my nephew. They killed kin to folks I know and like. The reasons don't matter. Not now. What matters is seein' to it it don't happen any more than it's got to. The only way to do that is make your stand. This is mine. I'm too old to care about anything but protecting what's mine."

Slocum didn't say anything, and Settle turned in the saddle to watch him closely. "You don't have to agree, son. But you got to understand."

Slocum nodded. "I understand."

"That's all a man can ask."

7

The small cavalry unit reined in fifty yards away. Vernon Settle, who had already exploded twice, and was showing no signs of regaining his composure, spurred his mount toward the five men in blue. Slocum was right on Settle's heels. He could hear the old man cursing over the pounding hooves.

"Jesus Christ, Lieutenant, you mean to tell me all Charlie Martin can spare is a handful of wet-behind-the-ears hooligans from back East and yourself, probably not even a Point man?"

The young lieutenant, taken aback by the assault, tossed a salute. Slocum guessed it was probably softer than what he would have preferred to throw. "Lieutenant Michael Rogers, Fifth Cavalry," he said. "Colonel Martin said you had some trouble."

"Trouble my foot, Lieutenant. We got the makings of a small war here. And we can't fight it with what you brung along, that's for damn sure."

"What exactly is the problem?"

"Problem? Can't you hear me, boy? We don't have a problem. We have an Indian uprising. Near twenty Apache bucks from who the hell knows where killed one of my men and run off over two hundred head of prime horseflesh. They tried to kill Slocum here," and at that he cocked a thumb over his shoulder, "and he got us even. But it ain't gonna stay even. Not unless we hit them hard while they're still around. You understand me, boy?"

"I'm trying, Mr. . . ."

"Settle, boy, Vernon Settle. Didn't he even tell you that much?"

"Mr. Settle. I'm trying to understand but you're not making it easy for me."

Settle threw up his hands, snatched at his reins, and wheeled his mount. "You tell him, Slocum. I'll bust a gut if I have to keep listening to him."

Settle goaded his mount and headed back toward the rest of his hands. Slocum sketched the details as clearly and concisely as he could. When he was finished, Rogers nodded, but didn't say anything.

"No questions?" Slocum asked.

Rogers shook his head. "Nope. Must be the renegades from over San Carlos. We knew they were heading this way. Didn't expect them to get here so soon, though."

"What do I tell Mr. Settle?"

"You know where they are?"

"He's got a good idea."

"Then let's get going. I don't want to run into them after nightfall." He paused a moment, then looked Slocum square in the eye. "And you don't either, that much I can tell you."

Slocum rode back to tell Settle what Rogers proposed. Instead of an answer, the old man spurred his mount, raised a fist in the air, and broke to the southwest. Rogers, as if he'd seen this sort of thing a thousand times before, just shook his head, then ordered his detachment to follow him.

The cavalrymen were laughing among themselves, for all the world as if they were off on some school picnic. For them, maybe it is, Slocum thought. But only for a moment. He hadn't been able to shake off the bloodcurdling echo of that solitary war cry as he lay among the rocks in the canyon through Broken Back Mesa. This was no picnic, and he wasn't sure Vernon Settle understood that. The question was, Would he understand it before it was too late?

Watching the old man push his mount, he didn't think so. That wasn't the way Vernon Settle was made. For all of his reason, the old man was running on rage now, and the man who had screamed at Lieutenant Rogers was not the man who talked so cogently about the situation the night before.

Two hours later, Settle jerked his horse to a halt and dropped from the saddle. Trailing the reins behind him in one fist, he moved cautiously ten, then fifteen feet. He let go of the reins and glanced back at Rogers. "Two hours, maybe less," he said.

"How do you know it's them?"

"Because I know, that's how. How in the hell you think I got to be this old out here, dammit? Them two bucks Slocum was following been by here, sure as I'm standin' here wastin' my time and precious breath." He walked back to his mount and swung easily into the saddle.

The first contact, however tenuous it might have seemed, sobered the four cavalrymen. Rogers seemed less impressed, but he was willing to give the old man as much rope as he needed to trip over. If he hung himself, that was all right, too.

They took it slower now, heading for the Florida Mountains. Settle seemed unconcerned, as if he had been looking forward to this meeting for most of his life. The others weren't so sure. The first flush of rage had cooled, and now reason was starting to suggest that maybe it was up to the Army, not a handful of angry cowhands, to punish the Apaches. But they knew that if they wanted to continue to work for Vernon Settle, they were in until the old man called a halt. It was that or find work someplace else.

The sun was harsh. Settle's horses were holding up reasonably well, but his men had a change of mounts. The Army horses were not doing nearly as well. Rogers knew it, but wanted Settle to see it for himself, instead of raising the issue. There was no point in giving the old man a platform for yet another tirade.

As the afternoon wore on, it was obvious to Slocum that the Apaches were being less careful. They might have been tired, or they might have been confident they had outstripped any pursuit. But there was another explanation, one that nibbled at the back of Slocum's mind like a mouse nibbling at a piece of cheese. Maybe the Apaches *wanted* to be followed. He kept trying to push the thought aside, but it wouldn't leave him alone.

Settle stayed at the head of the column, like some self-anointed Custer. Whenever anyone—Slocum included—got close, he'd push his horse a little harder. Whether he feared he was falling back, or whether he wanted to discourage any conversation, Slocum wasn't sure. Either way, somebody was going to have to say something. And soon.

The mountains were only two miles away now, and they had three hours of sun left. Rogers finally took the bit in his mouth. Catching Slocum's eye, he pointed toward Settle's broad back and urged his mount forward. Slocum followed. The lieutenant caught up, but Settle lashed his animal with the reins. Rogers was ready for him, dug his own spurs in, and got far enough ahead to turn his horse and confront the old man.

"Get out of the way, boy," Settle barked.

"No, sir. We got to talk, first."

"There's nothing to talk about. We know what we got to do. Let's just get it done so we can go on home."

"No, sir, not until we talk it over."

Settle sighed the sigh of a long-suffering father confronted by a wayward son yet again. But he nodded. "Speak your piece, so we can get on with it."

"You said there were about twenty of them, right?"

"Give or take."

"All right, let's say take. Let's say there's fifteen. I don't like the odds."

"We're pretty near even. What's wrong with the odds, Lieutenant?"

"For one thing, you might be wrong. They might not be

heading to Mexico. If they hole up in the Florida range, it might take us weeks to find them. We're not equipped for that. And there might be more of them. Suppose they didn't take those animals to sell. Suppose, just for a minute, they took them to keep. Suppose they're up there waiting for us."

"So what? They're my horses they took. It was one of my hands they killed—my nephew, in fact. Kin, you understand? You mean I'm supposed to let them off scot-free? That what you're telling me?"

"I'm not telling you anything, dammit. Just listen. I'm speculating. We have to be prepared for what we'll find."

"I am prepared, dammit. I'm prepared to find the sonofabitches killed Rick Hardee. More than that, I'm prepared to cut out their damn gizzards and cook 'em over an open fire. I am prepared to take back what's mine and go home. That's what I'm prepared for. What are you prepared for, Lieutenant?"

"Reality, Mr. Settle."

Settle snorted. "That what they call it nowadays? I thought the Army was supposed to protect citizens' rights. I thought it was supposed to keep them Apaches in line. I thought you were on my side, dammit. That's what I thought."

"No, you're not thinking at all. All you want to do is get revenge. But there's ways to do that without exposing your men and *my* men for no reason other than because you're too damn reckless to listen."

"What the hell you want us to do, Lieutenant, *ask* them if they'd mind coming back to San Carlos, stepping into a noose and jumping off a chair? I don't think that's too likely."

"No, that's not what I'm asking. I think we should confine ourselves to finding their encampment. To do that, we have to be cautious. I don't think there's anything to be gained by charging right up the mountain into their guns."

"Lieutenant, while we sit here, they're probably already putting ground between them and us. We don't have that much time. You know as well as I do that once they cross the border into Mexico, it'll take weeks, maybe months, to get permission from the Mexicans to cross the border. What chance you think we'll have then?"

"The treaty provides for hot pursuit, Mr. Settle. You probably know that."

"Sure, I know it. And I also know there's no way in hell you can call what we're doing hot pursuit. What we're doing is sitting here flapping our gums. That's all we're doing. Never yet seen an Apache scared of that. Have you boys?" He turned to look back at his men. They laughed nervously, but it was obvious the heart had gone out of them. They'd had too much time to think about what might happen.

And Settle knew it. He kicked his mount and swung past Rogers. Over his shoulder, he said, "You do what you want, Mr. Rogers. I'm gonna get them Apaches and I'm gonna do it now!"

Rogers shook his head. He'd seen stubborn ranchers before, but Vernon Settle was one for the books. He understood the old man's anger, even sympathized with it. But he had responsibilities Settle couldn't begin to grasp. Not only was he responsible for his men, he was under orders. He had to justify whatever he did to men who held his career, even his life, in the palms of their hands. Vernon Settle didn't have to worry about such things.

"Look, Mr. Settle, I—"

"No, you look, Lieutenant. I already told you what I think. I already told you what I'm going to do. Now, you can either come along, or you can go home. But don't even think about getting in my way. I won't have it. I won't allow it, do you understand?"

"Are you threat—"

Settle cut him off. "No, I'm not threatening you, Lieutenant. I'm just telling you how it is going to be. Now, I've made it about as plain as I can make it. Even an Army man ought to understand what I've just said. Do you?"

"Yes, sir, I do. But—"

Settle shook his head vehemently. "No, Lieutenant, there are no buts in New Mexico Territory. Not today, and not ever when it comes to Apaches." He turned away and kicked his mount. Rogers, uncertain of what to do, and by now convinced there was nothing he *could* do, followed reluctantly. He had a bad feeling about all this.

8

"Up there." Settle pointed to a notch between two oblique stone faces. "That's where they must have gone."

"That's their kind of territory," Lieutenant Rogers said.

"I know it. But if you want to beat the Apaches, you got to do it on their terms. They're tough, but they're also smart. We have to be tougher and smarter."

"I have responsibility for these men," Rogers reminded him.

"Hell, I know that. But I have responsibility for my men, too. Now, we can sit here with our hands in our pockets, we can turn tail, or we can show them who's boss."

"At what cost, Mr. Settle?"

"If we do it right, at no cost, Lieutenant. But nothing worth having comes cheap, unless you're smart about it. You see what I mean?"

"I think it's a mistake. Colonel Martin told me—"

"The hell with Charlie Martin. He ain't here, Rogers. *You* are. Now, did you ride all the way out here for nothing, like some damn spectator at a boxing match, or did you come ready to get your nose bloody, as an Army man? I can live with it either way. But either way, I am gonna get what's mine."

Slocum listened to the exchange without speaking. He knew what Settle was trying to do. Rogers knew it too.

But it didn't seem to make any difference. It was working. "Mr. Settle," he said, "I think maybe—"

"Hold it right there, Slocum. Soon as I hear that word 'maybe,' I know somebody's fixing to make excuses. I don't want excuses. I want my horses. I want the bastards killed my nephew. And I mean to have 'em, even if I have to go up there by myself. Now, we got more than an hour of sun left. Let's go, Rogers."

Rogers squeezed the air out of his lungs in a tight stream of exasperation. Then he nodded. "All right. But I think we should send a small team for reconnaissance purposes. I want to know exactly what we're up against."

"That's the new Army way, is it? I'm going myself, then. Slocum, you're coming with me."

Rogers picked one of his men, and the four of them dismounted. They were a quarter of a mile from the base of the formidable-looking mountain wall. Already, as the sun started to slip, it was wrapped in purple light. As they spread out in a wide line and started toward the base of the wall, Settle said, "They already know we're here. But that shouldn't make any difference."

"I hope not," Rogers whispered, more to himself than anyone else.

Sprinting in a ragged line four abreast, they reached the base of the wall, then moved laterally, looking for some way to climb the face. "There's a half dozen shallow valleys up in these mountains where you could hide a whole army," Rogers said. "If there's more of them than you think, we're in big trouble."

"Son," Settle laughed, "not half the trouble *they're* in. You got to think positive. Lieutenant. No room for drawing-room nerves here."

Slocum found a promising trail, and started up, the other three right behind him. The trail wound back and forth among the fractured rocks and fluted columns of reddish stone. It was steep, and the going was slow. But it beat taking the horses the long way around. That route was almost certainly heavily guarded. As it was, Slocum kept thinking they weren't even sure whether the Apaches were up there. But Settle was hardheaded, and nobody had a better thought.

They took turns watching the rocks above them, two sweeping the rimrock and the jumbled boulders lower down with the muzzles of their rifles while the other two moved ahead fifteen or twenty yards. Then they reversed roles. Leapfrogging through the mazelike passages, they found themselves more than a hundred feet in the air now. Slocum looked back and down. He could see the rest of them, still on their horses, their faces upturned, watching the painful progress.

So far, there was no indication they were being watched. Slocum, crouching behind a boulder, scanned the top half of the sloping wall with binoculars. In the slowly failing light, it was difficult to pick out the rocks from their shadows. He had the feeling they were wasting their time. Once night fell, they would be able to do nothing. And the Apaches, if they were there at all, would not attack during the night. That meant either finding their way back down in the darkness, or spending the night up top. Neither prospect was appealing.

Looking down again, he saw that the shadow of the mountain had crept closer to the waiting men, spilling across the flat, rocky ground like a dark flood. He dropped the glasses and turned to Rogers to wave him on to the next leg.

"Don't place too much stock in them glasses, Slocum," Settle said. "You won't see them unless they want to be seen. But they're there, all right."

As if to contradict him, a glint of light winked once, then a second time up toward the rim. To catch the sunlight, it had to be high up. Slocum pointed and Settle jerked his head around as Rogers broke into a run.

"What is it? What'd you see, Slocum?" The old man sounded almost happy, as if he had been looking forward to this for a long time, the way a kid waits for Christmas.

"Not sure. Light, a reflection, but I couldn't tell for sure from what."

"Give me them glasses." Settle held out his hand without turning around, and Slocum slapped them into the extended palm. "Where am I looking?"

Slocum squeezed alongside of the older man and pointed. "See that flat-topped rock, just a couple or three feet down? To the left of it."

Settle raised the field glasses, adjusted the focus with his index finger, and panned slowly back and forth. "Don't see anything," he grunted. "You sure?"

"I'm sure."

He watched Settle's face, the tongue jutting out and pinched between the old man's blocky teeth. The lips were clenched white with concentration. "Nothing, maybe you—"

A rock fell, off to the right, and Slocum glanced over just in time to see motion. What caused it, he couldn't tell. Then Rogers skidded in behind him, the enlisted man right behind him. "What's going on?"

"Slocum thinks he saw something," Settle whispered. "But he ain't sure what."

There was a hiss of sand, and it drifted down over them. Directly in front of them, a section of the face rose straight up some thirty feet. The face was studded with outcroppings of rock, and Settle handed the glasses back. He stood and moved toward the sheer face. "Watch the top of that damn wall," he said.

"Where the hell you going?" Rogers hissed.

Settle pointed straight up, but didn't say anything. A moment later, he was at the foot of the rock wall and planting his foot on a sharp rock formation. He hoisted himself then reached overhead to grab for a handhold. Spread-eagled against the rock, he raised his left leg, found secure footing, then levered himself up another two feet.

"Keep an eye up there," Rogers said, pointing. Slocum used the glasses, despite the short distance, hoping to catch some little sign. But the light was too far gone. The sky was starting to turn from blue to gray now, the clouds boiling off in the western sky now orange and blue-white as they tumbled across the Florida Mountains.

More sand sifted down. They heard it rattle on Settle's hat, and the old man had to look down to keep from getting it in his eyes. At the same instant, a shadow moved at the right-hand corner of the shelf. Slocum swung his gun around as the shadow backed away and disappeared.

"Vernon," he shouted. "Look out."

At the same instant, a rifle cracked. The bullet glanced off the top of the boulder and spanged away, scattering sharp slivers of rock. Slocum ducked instinctively, pulling Rogers down beside him.

"That was too damn close," the lieutenant muttered.

"You all right, Mr. Settle?" Slocum shouted.

"So far." He didn't sound frightened. His voice was the same mellow baritone. Another shot barked, and this time the bullet whined by without striking anything at all. Slocum still hadn't seen the shooter.

A sudden scraping sound, like that of a mausoleum being opened, drifted down from above. Slocum looked up in time to see a large rock teetering on the edge of the mountain rim. Small stones and clumps of dirt fell away from beneath it as the boulder rocked back and forth once, then again and a third time. It tipped forward, seeming to balance on a pinpoint.

"Vernon, hug the wall," Slocum shouted. "Above you!"

He sighted on the rock swirling his tongue against the back of his teeth. He felt his shoulders tighten. The rock still hung there motionless. The sand had stopped cascading now, and Vernon Settle, realizing what was happening, started to crab down the wall. In his haste, he lost one foothold and stabbed at the smooth rock with a booted foot, finally managing to catch something long enough to shift his weight.

The rock leaned over suddenly and Slocum tightened his

finger on the trigger. Rogers was scrambling toward the base of the wall. Settle, still twelve feet up, pushed back and dropped straight down. He landed hard, but Rogers grabbed him before he could fall.

Only vaguely aware of the scramble at the base of the sheer face, Slocum held his breath. The rock tipped forward now, abruptly falling outward, then scraped the rock face high above them. In a single instant, Slocum saw the splayed arms of an Apache, struggling to regain his balance now that the rock was no longer there.

He squeezed the trigger and saw the Indian stumble back a step, his arms folding over his chest as if he were hugging something Slocum couldn't see.

The falling rock started a thunderous cascade, breaking others free as it bounced down the mountain wall. Boulders of every size and shape dislodged by the huge rock, boulders that in turn dislodged others, swept the stone face in a widening rush. Slocum saw the Apache pitch forward now. The Indian fell silently, tumbling once, his arms still folded across his chest.

Settle, half-hauled by Rogers, staggered away from the oncoming landslide. Both men tumbled in behind Slocum and pressed themselves up against the large boulder, hoping to God it could withstand the impact of the falling stone.

One rock, the size of a man's head, slammed into the top of their cover and roared past Slocum's outstretched arm, narrowly missing it. A cloud of dust swirled ahead of the stone, choking the crouching men. Crash after crash shook their only protection and then the big rock glanced off the side of their own, shaking it, then rumbling past.

The huge boulder tumbled downhill, and Slocum peered through the swirling dust to watch. End over end now, it looked like an ungainly gymnast as it cartwheeled down the sloping face of the mountain wall, twice changing direction as it slammed into rocks half its size. Then, with a thud that seemed to shake the ground itself, it hit bottom. The thunderous impact rolled up past them echoing off the mountain, then died away. Now there was the titter of small stones and finally just the hiss of cascading sand.

Then quiet.

"I'll be damned," Settle whispered. "I'll be damned. Should have listened to you, Slocum. But don't you dare say you told me. I know it, and I don't want to hear about it."

"What now?" Rogers asked.

Vernon shrugged. "Well, I'd say we found them. Now we got to convince your boss he's got to do something about it."

9

Slocum sat on the bunkhouse porch, watching the sun rise. The smell of coffee, stronger than usual, hung in the air. Some of the hands were already heading out after an early breakfast. Vernon Settle had issued orders, in no uncertain terms, that the men were to ride the perimeter and report back the least hint that the Apaches might be planning to cut into his livestock.

"They think I'm an easy target now," he had grumbled. "Hell, part of me agrees with the bastards. But we'll show them."

It was likely the Apaches didn't need to be shown anything at all. There was little they hadn't seen from the white man, good or bad, and Slocum knew, as Vernon Settle did not want to admit, that nothing anyone could do would change the Apaches, or the white men either. They were what they were, both camps, and there was nothing personal in it for the Apaches. They were living the way they knew how.

Slocum got up slowly and walked toward the well, lowered the pail and cranked it back up. He set the pail down, leaned over for the battered ladle, and scooped it full of the cold, clear water. After a second sip, he poured the rest back, listened to the echoing splash and looked toward the main house.

Someone was watching him through the front window, he was certain. He squinted in the morning light, but all he could see was the bunched curtain pulled aside just far enough for a slit of light. While he watched, the curtain fell again. A moment later, Ginny Settle was on the front porch. She waved, and stepped off the broad stairs and headed toward him, her hands tucked in the back pockets of her jeans.

She was tall, maybe five nine, Slocum guessed. Her light brown hair was pulled back behind her ears and held in place by a pair of silver barrettes which caught the reddish sunlight as she moved, and sent tiny red spears off into the sky. Her face was solemn, but even so he could see just how pretty she was. A handful of freckles dusted her nose, and her eyes, big and dark, shone brightly. Her figure had turned more than one head on the spread, and Slocum himself had wondered why she wasn't married yet. At twenty-four, beautiful and the daughter of one of the wealthiest men in the territory, she was more than an average catch. But she was, after all, Slocum thought, Vernon Settle's "little girl," and that would explain quite a lot.

"Mr. Slocum," she said, still several yards away.

"Miss Settle, morning."

"Can I talk to you a minute?"

"The boss's daughter can do just about anything she wants, I guess."

Ginny laughed. It was rich and throaty, and her smile was full. "One of the advantages," she said.

"What do you want to talk about?"

"The boss . . ."

"I think you got the wrong man, Miss Settle. I'm new here, and even if I wasn't, it's not my place to be talking about the man who pays my wages. Even with his daughter. Maybe *especially* with his daughter."

"I don't mean to compromise you in any way, Mr. Slocum, but I have to talk to someone."

"Why me?"

"Because you're . . . well, different. You're not like the other hands."

Slocum nodded. "All right . . ."

"Not here." She walked toward the barn. He followed after her, wondering why she wanted to talk in the barn, but she moved on past and out into the open field beyond it. She was moving fast, and he had to lengthen his stride to keep up. There was a small brook in the meadow bottom, outlined by willows and cottonwoods on one bank, and she didn't slow down until she reached it.

Finally, she sat down on a sandy bank, snatched a fistful of stiff grass, and drummed on the tight denim of her muscled thigh. "Sit down," she said.

Slocum did as he was told, growing more curious by the second. "Anything wrong?" he asked.

"You tell me," she said.

"I'm afraid I can't tell you anything you don't already know."

"You were with my father the last couple of days. I know that. And I also know he talked to you one night. He told me that. He seems to think very highly of you. He didn't say what you talked about, but . . ."

"Then I guess he didn't want you to know, Miss Settle."

"I'm not asking you to betray a confidence, Mr. Slocum. It's just that I'm worried about him. He doesn't seem quite right, somehow. I can't explain it, really, but I know there's something wrong."

"He lost some horses. One of his men, family at that, was killed. I think he took it pretty hard. That's probably all."

"No," she snapped, "it isn't." She slapped the grass so hard against her leg the blades snapped. "You men are all alike. You think you have to keep secrets. You think it makes you stronger than anybody else."

"No, ma'am, that's not the case. It's just that if there's anything bothering Mr. Settle, he didn't tell me about it. He was just talking, that's all. Not about anything in particular. He mentioned how you were all he had left since your mother died. I think it made him kind of sad, and he closed up pretty quickly. It seemed almost like he was embarrassed to talk about it. I suppose a thing like that has to be painful, and he's worried about you. About your future. He knows he won't live forever."

"He acts like he will."

"Men do that, I'll grant you. You have to understand something, Miss Settle, not just about your daddy, but about life out here."

"I was born and raised here, Mr. Slocum. Just because I went to school back East doesn't mean I'm a stranger to this territory. I know what it's like, how hard it is, how it can grind you down. But that's just the point, don't you see? The harder you push, the more it grinds you down. Just like sharpening a knife. My father is pushing too hard."

"It isn't that simple, Miss Settle. There's a lot more to it than that. If you don't push at all, the knife doesn't get sharp. You got to push some."

She changed the subject abruptly. "You know what he's doing today?"

"No, ma'am, I don't. I'm just a hired hand. Your father doesn't tell me anything I don't need to know to do my job."

"And what is your job, Mr. Slocum?"

"I'm a ranch hand, Miss Settle, no more and no less. I am not a confessor or a confidant. Like I told you, I just happened to be there. I couldn't sleep and neither could he. He opened up a little and closed up right away. That doesn't change what I am or what I know."

"Well, I'll tell you what he's doing today, since you claim not to know."

Slocum held up a hand. "Hold on, Miss Settle, if he wanted me to know, I'm sure he'd tell me."

Ginny nodded. "You're right. He would. But you see, Mr. Slocum, *I* want you to know, and that's why I'm telling you. He's trying to convince the other ranchers to put a small army together to go back after the Apaches, with soldiers from Fort Stillwell."

"I can understand that."

"Can you really?" The tone was so acidic, Slocum wondered whether it had burned her lips.

She lay back on the sand, her hands behind her head. He noticed her breasts, then caught her looking at him, and wondered whether he was supposed to notice them. The posture seemed almost calculated.

"Have you ever been married, Mr. Slocum?"

"No, ma'am. But—"

"Because I was wondering what my father must be thinking, about me being his only family, I mean. I guess if you measure your accomplishments by the number of children you leave behind, having just one must seem like failure."

"I wouldn't know."

"You ever think about having a family?"

"Sometimes." The truth was, he'd thought about it a lot, but it was none of her business, and he didn't see where the conversation was going. It made him uneasy.

"I think about it."

Slocum nodded.

"But I don't think I ever will. I don't think I'll ever get married. Men are such fools."

Slocum said nothing.

"Do you think I'm pretty?"

"Is that what you brought me down here to find out?"

"No, but I noticed you looking at me, and since you don't want to tell me what I really want to know, I thought I might as well get something out of the trip. If you think I'm pretty, that is. If not, I'd as soon you kept your opinion to yourself."

"And you say men are fools," Slocum laughed. "Seems to me like there's nothing more foolish than living your life by what other people think of you. If you think you're pretty, then you are, no matter what I think."

"Even if I were ugly?"

"You're not."

"But if I were?"

"Even then," he said. "Pretty is inside, too."

"Will you do me a favor, Mr. Slocum?"

"Depends on what it is, I guess."

"Will you try to talk my father out of going after those Apaches?"

"It's not my place to do that, Miss Settle."

"It is if I ask you to do it."

"You don't pay my wages, ma'am."

"But my father does."

"Is that what they taught you back East? How to throw your weight around?"

"That's not fair."

"Neither is you asking me to do that. Neither is bringing me out here and asking me whether you're pretty or not."

"Touché."

"If you don't mind, ma'am, I think I better get on back."

She didn't seem to have heard him. Then, after a long pause, she rolled over onto one hip and slapped at his knee with the remnants of the bunched grass. "Will you wait here while I take a quick swim?"

"No, ma'am, I won't."

"Afraid?"

"Of what?"

"You know damn well what I mean, Mr. Slocum." She sat up, tossed the grass into the brook, and looked him square in the eye. "Don't you?"

10

It had been a tense two days. Rumors were thick for fifty miles in every direction. A constant stream of visitors had poured through the Settle house, some to offer to join a reprisal raid, others to offer their moral support and caution Vernon to go carefully. Vernon welcomed the former like long-lost brothers. The latter he shunned as if they carried the plague. For some reason that Slocum couldn't understand, the old man was growing more resolute in his determination to exact some sort of revenge. It almost seemed as if he had lost sight of everything but getting even.

Now they were ready. Slocum, against his better judgment, was going along. Vernon had asked, and when Slocum declined, Vernon had ordered him. He didn't have much more than his horse and what it could carry, so he knuckled under.

Using all his influence in the territorial capital, Vernon had managed to put enough pressure on Colonel Charles Martin to pry a twenty-man column out of Fort Stillwell. At Settle's insistence, Lieutenant Rogers was to be second in command. "Got to teach that boy a few things before he gets us all killed," was how Vernon explained his curious request. But his long acquaintance with Martin and his not inconsiderable clout in the capital had combined to get him what he wanted.

The plan was simple. Settle, at the head of a column of ranchers and ranch hands, would meet the cavalry unit at the mouth of Copper Canyon. He was convinced now that the Indians hadn't run, and he was determined to hang them all, if he couldn't manage to shoot them first. They had two miles to go, and Slocum had been watching the dust kicked up by the Army horses for more than two hours. The dust hung in the air like a cloud that shadowed not only the ground but all of reality. The attack made no sense, but Slocum seemed to be the only one willing to say so. He resented being forced to participate, but he finally decided that he might be able to talk Vernon out of the worst of his rage. For that reason alone, he had finally consented.

They joined on the military column at a few minutes after noon. Settle had already briefed the unit commander, a rangy captain named Byron Belcher, on the layout of the Apache stronghold. The Florida Mountains stuck up out of the ground as if they had been carved out of whole stone and physically placed there in a single piece. They were more a collection of steep-faced mesas than real mountains, but harboring dozens of valleys full of rich grass and clear ponds fed by springs. The overflow from the ponds formed a single stream that meandered among the shallow, bowllike valleys and spilled down the southern side of the small range and gradually wound its way to the Mimbres River.

With a large enough force, Settle was convinced he could force the narrow, sloping canyon that gave the only easy access to the heart of the stronghold. And he was prepared to lose a few men to prove his point. Belcher, unused to taking orders from anyone but an Army officer, resented Settle's interference, but he had been told to accommodate the old man, and he knew better than to buck a direct order. He'd worked hard for his bars, and he'd be damned if he'd lose them for so foolish a reason as common sense.

Belcher had three White Mountain Apache scouts with his unit, and he'd already sent them ahead before Settle and his men arrived. Now, all he wanted to do was wait for the scouts to return before drawing up a battle plan that would protect his men and at least give Settle some semblance of what he wanted.

Most white men were in the habit of thinking of the Apaches as a monolithic horde of barbarous savages. But the reality was far different. There were eight or ten different tribes loosely collected under the name Apache, and some, like the Warm Spring Apaches, were as bitter enemies of others, like the Bedonkohe, as any two white men. The White Mountain Apaches were relatively friendly to the whites, and had no use for the Chiricahua or the Bedonkohe. Cochise, Mangas, Geronimo and Nana, those best known to white men, and whose very names were enough to send women and children to hide in the root cellar, were as hated by some Apaches as they were by whites.

But these were distinctions that most whites didn't bother to make. An Apache was an Apache was the conventional wisdom, and that meant an Indian who at best deserved a rope, with or without trial, and then only when there was no way to save the territory the cost of a trial right from the git go.

As Belcher refused to budge until his scouts returned, Vernon Settle paced restlessly beside his horse. Slocum noticed the old man's nervousness, and slipped alongside to try to calm him down.

"It makes sense, Mr. Settle," he said. "No reason we can't wait another hour, if it will save lives."

"I'm not interested in saving lives, Slocum. You know that."

"Yeah, I do. What I don't know is why."

Settle sighed. "You're too young to understand."

"Try me."

"Look, I been here for more than thirty years. When I first came, Mimbres was three buildings, and you had to go outside to sneeze in every one of them, if you didn't want to blow out a wall. I scratched until my hands were bloody. I built everything I had, carrying lumber fifty miles in a wagon to build my house and my barn. My daughter was born here. My wife died here. You know what that's like? Sweating like that, bleeding like that, so you can have someplace to call your own?"

"I have an idea, yeah."

"Then you ought to understand how it sticks in my craw that somebody wants to take it all away from me. And don't you make no mistake, that's what this is all about. Them Apaches want to run me and every other man with a white skin clean out of this country. If they can't kill us and leave us to rot for the buzzards, that is. I won't have it, Slocum. Never. Not as long as I can curl my finger around a trigger, I won't. You better believe it."

"I believe it, Mr. Settle."

"But . . . ?"

"But I think there's more to it than you're telling me."

Settle smiled disarmingly. "There's that, too," he said. "There's that too."

Slocum was about to push a little harder, but a shout went up from the fringe of the waiting column. "Riders comin'."

"We'll talk again, Slocum," Settle said. "I got to get to that brass-polishing monkey to make sure he does what he's supposed to."

Slocum followed him through the milling men and horses. As he stepped clear, he could see the small cloud two miles away. By the look of it, it couldn't be more than two men, three at the most. Almost certainly the White Mountain scouts. They closed in a hurry, and skidded to a halt at the head of the column. Settle sprinted toward Belcher, who was still sitting on his horse as one of the Apaches dismounted.

The scout spoke fairly good English, and was already explaining what they'd found by the time Slocum got within earshot.

"You're sure about that?" Belcher was asking.

The scout nodded. "Empty."

"No one there at all, no women, even, no old men?"

"No one. Just wickiups, all empty, and horses."

"Let's get moving," Settle said, tugging on Belcher's reins. "Those're my horses."

"You don't know that, Mr. Settle."

"Then whose could they be?"

"They could belong to anybody."

"Then let's go check them out. My mustangs were already branded when they was run off. We can find out quick enough. You can read a brand, can't you?"

"Yes, Mr. Settle, I can."

"Then what are we waiting for?"

"My orders were to engage the Apache renegades. There are none here."

"But they *were* here. It's the same thing."

"Past tense, Mr. Settle."

"We're going up there. Now, you can either come along and do what you're supposed to do, or we'll go ourselves. But I guarantee you, when I get back, I'll see to it you are court-martialed. They'll bury you so deep, you'll be closer to China than New Mexico. Do you understand?" Without a backward glance, Settle stormed toward his horse and swung into the saddle.

He charged ahead, the rest of the ranchers and cowhands falling in behind him, in a headlong gallop. Belcher looked at Slocum, who shrugged helplessly and moved to his own mount.

They covered the distance to the mouth of Copper Canyon in fifteen minutes. Settle called a halt just long enough to shout, "If you believe them scouts, there's nobody home. That means we got nothing to worry about. But if I was you, I'd keep an eye peeled." With that, he spurred his horse and charged up the sloping floor of the canyon, keeping to the middle and swiveling his head from side to side to watch the rimrock on either side.

The canyon opened into a flat-bottomed valley. It was empty of everything but grass and an occasional boulder. Settle bulled ahead, racing up the ridge dead ahead and on down into the next valley. At the far end, Slocum, who was now in the middle of the column, could see a cluster of wickiups, fifteen or eighteen at the most. Behind the wickiups, the ground rose more sharply, except to the left, where another canyon joined this one at an angle.

They started firing their weapons in the air and shouting. It struck Slocum as bizarre. There didn't seem to be a soul in the Apache rancheria. Not even a wisp of smoke suggested the camp had recently been inhabited.

Settle ordered the ranchers to burn the wickiups, then charged on into the next valley, a Colt Peacemaker clutched in one fist. He fired a couple of rounds, then let out a whoop.

"My horses," he shouted. "My horses."

Slocum charged ahead, catching up to the old man just as he leapt from the saddle and sprinted toward a makeshift corral of mesquite branches tied together with braided vines. Settle sprinted to a large rock and clambered up and over the mesquite to plunge down among the restless mustangs. He chased a yearling down and checked the brand. Slocum stayed in the saddle just beyond the fence.

Settle turned with a grin. "They're mine, Slocum," he said. "I told you. I knew it. I *knew* it. Now, you tell me it wasn't worth the trouble."

"Why is it this easy, Mr. Settle?"

"What? Speak up, boy. Old men are hard of hearing, don't you know that?"

"I asked you why you thought it was this easy."

"Who cares. You don't ask questions like that. You just take what's yours and thank the Lord."

"I'm not so sure, Mr. Settle."

"You're a damn pessimist, Slocum."

"I hope you're right."

"I know it. I know you are. Damn. Looks like ever' last one of them is here."

"Now, all we got to do is get them out of here," Slocum said.

"Boy, maybe I misjudged you. I thought you had real sand. I thought you were a throwback, Slocum, like the men I come here with, like the men who made this civilized country. Looks like I was wrong."

"No, you weren't wrong. But I think you're making a big mistake. In fact, I think it's already too late. We're in, and I'll bet a month's pay we have a tougher time getting out."

"Son, I rode through that damned canyon same as you. I was watching the rim, same as you. I didn't see nobody, Indian or white, up there. Did you?"

"No, I didn't, but that doesn't—"

"Son, it means there's no damned Apaches here. We scared them off. That's what it means. Now, let's just get what's ours and go home."

11

Settle was ecstatic. He kept laughing and poking Belcher in the ribs with a thick finger. "You see, Captain, you see? I told you, didn't I?"

Belcher was less certain there was cause for celebration. "Mr. Settle, as far as I can tell, your happiness might be just a little premature."

"Why? I got my horses back, and we come out whole, didn't we?"

"So far, yes."

"And that's the way it's gonna stay, Captain. That's the way it's gonna stay."

"You wonder where the Apaches are, do you, Mr. Settle? Because I do."

"I don't care. They're not here, that's what matters. Now, if you'll excuse me, I got some horses to drive." Belcher shook his head, then turned to the business of reorganizing his column.

Settle moved off a way and gathered the motley assortment of ranchers and hands around him and smiled broadly. "That's it, boys, we done it. All we got to do now is get them horses moving. Lafe, you take a couple of the boys and get in behind them mustangs. We'll cut that piddly little fence and you run 'em through. Let's hop to it, because I can tell the Army is anxious to get on home." The men laughed, and Settle pointed to Belcher. "The captain there thinks we ain't home free yet, so let's go along with him and see can we get out of here in one piece. 'Course, anybody wants to get shot here, he's gonna have to do it himself." The men laughed again, but Slocum didn't join them.

Belcher obviously was conservative, but there was something odd about the deserted rancheria that kept pulling at Slocum. It didn't make sense. Why abandon the camp and the horses? If the Apaches were moving on, they wouldn't have left their belongings, such as they were, behind. Especially not the horses. But if they hadn't headed south, where were they?

Slocum looked at the still-burning wickiups, at the columns of thick black smoke climbing a few hundred feet then spreading out, filling the valley with a pale gray haze. The sun was muted, and the shadows on the ground looked pale, their edges blurred by the reduced light.

Lafe Hedges picked a couple of hands, and the three men climbed in among the muttering animals. They seemed nervous, more nervous than they should have, and Slocum kept searching the ridges around the valley, looking for some sign they were not alone. But he found nothing.

Settle moved to the tangled fence of the improvised corral and started hacking at the braided vines with a big pocketknife. The vines were tough, and the mesquite did its best to scratch and rip at the old man's hide. When he had cut the ties through in several places, he pocketed the knife, ignoring the smears of blood on the backs of his hands, and started hauling the fence aside.

Slocum worked at the other end of a broad stretch of fence. They wanted a wide gap to keep the animals from trying to squeeze through too narrow an opening in their excitement. The valley was long enough that by the time they reached the other end, the animals would have had time to settle down. When he had finished cutting his section, Slocum looked at Settle.

"You nervous about something, Slocum?"

"Yes, sir, Mr. Settle, I am."

"You agree with that sorry-assed captain, don't you?"

Slocum nodded. He still hadn't seen anything unusual on the ridges surrounding them, but he couldn't shake the uneasy feeling. Settle grinned at him, and waved a hand dismissively. "Forget about it, son. We're almost finished here. You ready?"

"All set," Slocum said as he started to tug the mesquite aside.

"Watch me, Lafe," Settle shouted. "Soon as Slocum here is done, I'll give you the signal." He turned to the rest of the hands, who were already mounted, waiting for the mustangs to start their break through the opening.

Slocum looked around and noticed that Belcher had his men in a double column. The captain kept swiveling his head like an anxious bird. On his skinny neck, the head almost looked like it might wobble and fall off. He felt Slocum's gaze and turned. Slocum shook his head and Belcher shrugged.

"Okay, Mr. Settle, all done."

" 'Bout time, boy." He backed away from the opening, waited for Slocum to get clear, then cupped his hands and shouted, "Let 'er rip, Lafe."

Slocum sprinted for his horse, which was held by one of the other hands. The first few horses moved toward the opening tentatively, as if they suspected a trick. Lafe and his men started shouting and clapping their hands, and the animals in the back started to press forward. Gunshots would have been easier, but they didn't want to risk a stampede. They'd have to chase the herd for miles before getting it under control.

Settle was in the saddle and rode to the edge of the opening and stayed there, shouting and waving his hat, slapping it against his thigh while tugging on the reins to keep his own horse under control. The first horses finally pushed out into the open and, spurred on by Settle's ruckus, they turned and started down the valley. Following their lead, the rest of the horses bulled toward the break in the fence, shouldering one another aside where the gap narrowed a little, then spreading out and thundering down the gentle slope.

Settle's men peeled off one at a time, riding side by side with either edge of the herd. As the last stragglers burst clear, Lafe and his men raced after them and swung onto their waiting mounts. Slocum and Settle brought up the rear.

Slocum heard Belcher barking commands to his column, and the rattle of sabers as the cavalry unit started to move. He was pushing his horse, but glanced back to see the double column hit its stride, looking more like some monstrous brown and blue centipede than twenty men. The precision was remarkable, and it brought Slocum back for a second to the war. There was something about combat soldiers in motion that stayed with him all those years, and it didn't take much to trigger memories, fond and otherwise.

Turning his attention to the business at hand, he passed Settle and moved down along the left edge of the herd, which had hit its stride, too. The thunderous hooves filled the valley with a roar that drowned out everything now. Like dark water, the animals rushed downslope toward the second valley. The hands had all they could do to keep up, let alone stay in control. The mustangs had been branded, but they were anything but broken.

The gap into the second, larger valley loomed ahead. Wings of stone pinched the opening on either side, and the herd changed shape like a living thing to ooze through. It slowed things a little, and gave the hands a chance to catch their breaths. Then, as the gap opened out on the other side, the herd spurted through, gushing like water through a narrow spout, picked up speed for a moment, then fell back to a steady gallop.

Slocum glanced up at the rim. The walls here were much higher and more nearly vertical. On horseback, it was hard to fix his eye on any one thing, but he scanned the left side anxiously, as best he could.

Seeing nothing out of the ordinary, he started to relax. Lafe was just ahead of him, maybe twenty yards. Slocum watched as he rode his saddle as if he and his horse were a single living thing. Then, suddenly, Lafe missed a beat. He jerked sidewise, and turned his head.

"You hear anything?" he shouted, looking at Slocum. But the words were drowned out by the pounding hooves. He wheeled his horse in a tight circle, then fell in alongside Slocum. Cupping his hands into a megaphone, he shouted again. "You hear anything?"

Slocum shook his head.

Up front, Ray Collins, one of Settle's neighbors, turned his head toward the right and looked up at the rim. Slocum noticed and turned his gaze in the same direction.

What he saw made his blood run cold. Strung out like a picket fence dead ahead, almost evenly spaced over three hundred yards, nearly two dozen Apaches stood on the rim-rock. They were firing down into the canyon, but the waves of sound from the pounding hooves drowned out the reports.

As Slocum watched, three horses reared up, slapping at the sky with their hooves, then disappeared under the tid-al wave of horseflesh. The Indians were killing the mus-tangs.

Slocum leaned forward and grabbed his Winchester. Lafe saw the motion as Slocum roared past, and when he looked up, he, too, saw the Indians. Two hundred feet in the air, they were firing randomly, less interested in specific targets than in decimating the herd.

As more and more animals went down under the stag-gered fire, the herd started to divide into separate streams. They were swerving to avoid fallen animals, some of which were still struggling to regain their feet. Slocum headed for some cover and skidded to a halt. Out of the saddle before his mount stopped moving, he threw himself to the sandy ground then scrambled to a sitting position, his back against a boulder.

He fired once, twice, then a third time. Settle seemed to

realize what was happening only slowly. Slocum caught a glimpse of the old man, still on his horse, his mouth wide open in a soundless yell. The mounted column came to a halt as the horses thundered on. Belcher, drawing his sword in some foolish gesture he must have recalled only dimly from a West Point drill, waved the bright arcing blade at the sky. His men drew their weapons and started firing at the Apaches.

As the fire grew heavier, the Indians grew more cautious. One by one, they dropped to the ground, presenting virtually no target to the men trapped below. They were no longer firing at the horses. One of Belcher's men was hit. Slocum saw the bright geyser of blood where the bullet struck a young private in the shoulder. The wounded man fell from the saddle. As if it were a signal, the others dismounted and scrambled for the boulders along the base of the wall.

The hands with Settle, seeing what was happening, broke for the open country. Half of them were already past the Apache guns. They were home free, and they knew it. But Settle was made of something tougher. He wheeled his big stallion and charged back toward the scattered cavalrymen.

Belcher was doing his best to rally his troops, but the Apaches were already beginning to drift back away from the rim. Two more soldiers had been hit, and one, hit in the head, was certainly killed.

The Army men fired wildly, more concerned with getting off as many shots as they could than with where they were aiming. Almost as quickly as it had begun, it was over. Belcher seemed to realize it and called for a cease-fire. A few final cracks, accompanied by plumes of gray smoke, spat from the Army rifles, then they fell silent.

In the distance, Slocum could hear the horses pounding down through the mouth of the valley and across the open flats. A single moan drifted upward with the smoke, and Belcher sprinted to the side of the wounded private, still lying in the open. He shouted over his shoulder, "You men stay down. They could come back."

Slocum raced into the open and joined Belcher at the side of the wounded man. A pool of glossy blood had seeped from the wound and lay glistening on the ground. In its center, Slocum could see the reflected sun, so bright it hurt his eyes. The man was still conscious, but barely so.

"We have to stop the bleeding," Slocum said.

Belcher lost it momentarily. "I know that. Don't tell me my business." He whirled on Slocum then, his eyes refocusing only slowly. He shook his head. "Sorry," he said.

Slocum nodded. He took a bandanna from around his neck and shook out the dust. While Belcher lifted the man, Slocum bound the bullet wound as best he could, slipping Belcher's yellow neckerchief, folded into a thick pad, inside the back of the shirt then tying everything tightly.

He looked up as if something were calling to him. For a moment, outlined against the blue-white sky, a single Apache, his red headband bleached almost pink by the bright sunlight, stepped back and disappeared.

12

Settle fumed for three days. He hadn't lost a man, but Belcher had lost two killed and two severely wounded. There was some doubt whether the private Slocum had bandaged would survive.

But that didn't seem to bother the old man. What got under his saddle was the horses. One hundred and nineteen mustangs had escaped the slaughter. The Apaches had killed more than fifty outright, and several others had had to be destroyed. Whenever Slocum saw him, he would turn away, as if Slocum were somehow a reminder of a mistake he'd rather not remember.

On the morning of the fourth day, Slocum caught him early, sitting on the porch of the big house, an unlit pipe cupped in both hands. The old man saw him coming, and started to get up.

"You can run, but you can't change what happened, Mr. Settle."

Vernon moved to the door, opened it, then stopped. Looking back over his shoulder, he said, "You trying to tell me something, Slocum? Because if you are, I don't want to hear it."

"You don't have to listen, Mr. Settle, but I'm going to speak my piece, whether you like it or not. Now, either you can be man enough to sit back down and hear me out, or you can run inside and pretend like nothing happened. But that won't change a thing. Those two boys are dead, and no amount of pretending they aren't will let them draw another breath."

Settle let the screen door hit him in the back as Slocum planted himself at the bottom of the porch stairs. "If you want, I'll just stand here and shout. There's nothing you can do about it, either, except maybe fire me. But I'll tell you what, Mr. Settle, I won't work for a man who can't admit he made a mistake, and that's just what you did. Now, what's it gonna be? Are we going to talk this out, or are you going to pretend you're the only man in the great big world you told me about?"

There was no answer for a long moment. Slocum was conscious of movement beyond the screen, but he couldn't tell who it was or what was being done. A moment later, a large hand pressed against the screen, more in a posture of rest than of an attempt to open the door.

Finally, Settle reopened the door and walked out to the top step, where he sat down. "I'm listening," he said. "But I'm warning you, the first stupid thing you say, I'm going on back inside, and if that happens, I won't be coming back out, this time."

"Fair enough. First off, you know damn well we never should have gotten involved in this thing. You're no general. The Army knows how to handle these things, you don't. I know you're angry, and I know you want to just reach out and grab something by the neck. You'd like nothing more than to get your hands on some Apache buck and twist his head right off his shoulders. But that isn't the way it's going to be."

"You're getting close to stupid, boy."

"The hell I am. I'm right and you know it, whether you want to admit it or not."

In spite of himself, Settle asked a question. "What was I supposed to do? Write off them mustangs? Am I raising stock for any damn Indian with a gun to come along and take it? Is that what you think this is all about?"

"Of course not. But as far as what happened, yes, you should have written off those mustangs, or at least let the Army try and get them back."

"How am I supposed to run a business, I let the Apaches run off all my profits?"

Slocum shook his head. "This isn't about profits. This is about pride, plain and simple. Pride and something else. I don't know what that something else is, but it's there, in the background somewhere."

"That sounds suspiciously like an excuse. It okay with you if, come payday, I give you an excuse instead of thirty dollars? That seem like a good bargain to you?"

"If it's a good excuse, sure. I'll get my money eventually. What about those two boys killed out there? What can you give them?"

"I can say a prayer for 'em."

"Have you?"

"Of all the damn—"

"Have you, Mr. Settle?"

He shook his head. "No, I haven't. It won't help them none."

"I didn't think so."

"So what do you want from me?"

"What I want is an explanation. You don't think Rick Hardee was unlucky. You think he was killed on purpose, specifically him. And so do I."

"That all? You want me to tell you why?"

"Yes."

Settle patted the top step beside him. "Come on up here and have a seat. I'm not sure I can make this clear, and I'm only going to say it once, so you pay attention and you stop me if you don't understand something."

Slocum climbed the stairs. When he took a seat, he heard something inside the screen door and turned to look. Settle, without bothering to look, said, "Ginny, you get on out here where I can see you."

The door squeaked and Virginia Settle stepped onto the porch. Vernon turned to glare at her. "I told you before, I don't want you poking your nose into my business. I got enough to do without checking to see if you're butting in where you don't belong."

"I wasn't poking my nose in, Daddy. I was just interested, that's all. If you don't want me to listen, I'll go back inside." She was watching Slocum the whole time she spoke.

"No, sir," Settle said. "You go on over to the barn and stand there in the doorway, where I can keep an eye on you."

"Daddy!"

"Move!" Settle slapped the porch with a horny palm. The report sounded like a gunshot, and Ginny flinched. She stamped her foot, but another baleful glare from her father evaporated whatever resistance she had left. Reluctantly, dragging her feet like a girl half her age, she came down the stairs and crossed to the barn, where she turned and glared back, her arms folded across her chest. She made it plain she was obeying only under protest.

"Women," Settle said. He shook his head. "Just like her mama, that one is. Hardheaded, spiteful, can't stand to be left out of things. Her mother couldn't either."

"She's got a lot of heart," Slocum offered.

"Spite, I call it. Anyway, where was I?"

"You know damn well."

"All right." Settle straightened up and leaned out with one hand to grab onto one of the porch columns. "I been hearing stories, going on three years, now."

"What kind of stories?"

"Oh, this and that. About the Apaches mostly, about where they're getting their guns, where they're getting their horses, that sort of thing. Seems they got some friends with white skins, men who are playing both ends against the middle."

"What's that got to do with Hardee?"

"I'm not sure, not really. But I know it wasn't an accident

they run off those horses. I think somebody let them know about those horses. And I think maybe it was Rick. I can't prove it, but he'd been flashing money in town, money I ain't paid him. It hurts me to say that, him being my sister's boy and all, but I got to be truthful about it. I paid him more than I paid the other hands, so I know what he was making, but it wasn't anywhere near the money he was spending. I don't know where he got the rest of it, but I know he had it and I know it would be worth more than a few dollars to somebody if them Apaches kicked up a fuss every now and again. The more ruckus, the more Army, the more Army, the more money."

"For who?"

"For them who supply the Army, for starters. Think about it, Slocum. What happens if everything's nice and peaceful? What happens if your business is dependent on selling to the boys in blue, and they go home?"

Slocum nodded. "Would Hardee do that?"

"Sure he would. Hell, half the hands in this territory would do it. They like their drink and they like their women and they need money for both. If they can't come by an honest dollar, well a dishonest dollar will do. But, like I said, that's all supposing. I can't prove it."

"I still don't understand why you insisted on going after the horses yourself."

"Two reasons. Number one, it stuck in my craw to lose them. I can be bullheaded as the next man. I won't deny that. But the other reason was I wasn't sure but what if we found those mustangs we just might find a white man with them. Maybe the Apaches run them off, sell them to somebody for short change and the buyer changes the brand and resells 'em at a big profit. That's why I was in a hurry. Whoever he was, he wouldn't hang around too long, you got to realize that. Anybody found out who it was, he'd be swinging from a tree until there wasn't nothing but rope and bones."

"I see."

"Do you, Slocum? Can you really see it? Look, I told you the other night, my whole life is wrapped up in this place. And what *I* see is somebody trying to take it away from me. I'd hate for that to happen, and I won't sit by and let it happen if there's one damn thing I can do to stop it."

Slocum mulled it over. He was convinced Settle was telling the truth, but he felt disappointed somehow. He had thought, even hoped, that there would be an answer in the old man's explanation, but all he found was more questions. And he already had enough of those to keep him busy.

"Slocum, one thing. I don't want you to think I'm a heartless old fool who can't see past the drawstring on his pocketbook. I'm sorry for what happened to them two boys, and to Rick, and all that. I truly am. But there's some things a man has got to put his foot down on. I'm no different than anybody else. You said it was pride. Damn right it was. But without that, a man's nothing. And if he's nothing, he don't leave nothing behind, either. Might as well go in the ground now, as leave no sign you was even here. Maybe you're too young to understand that, but that's how it is."

Slocum was about to answer when he heard a gunshot out in the flats. Settle heard it too, and Ginny came running from the barn.

A rider was coming in hard. As he drew closer, he fired again. Settle jumped to his feet. "That's Red Kennedy," he said. "What the hell is he so bothered about?"

Kennedy nearly fell from his horse as he reined in, and Ginny realized he'd been hurt. She held a hand to her mouth. "Oh my God! He's all bloody," she shrieked.

"Ginny," Settle said, pushing his daughter behind him. "Get some water and bandages," he said over his shoulder. Then he helped the hand down from his horse, and dropped to one knee to lay the injured man on the ground.

"Red, what the hell happened?"

"Apaches, Vern. You got to help, quick. There's a bunch of them. They jumped the work detail. It's bad, and gonna get worse." He swallowed hard, then lay back and closed his eyes. His breathing was shallow, and his skin looked almost satiny white under its tan.

"Slocum, you get on out there, now. I'll be along as soon as I can."

13

Slocum vaulted over the corral fence as Settle raced into the house. He saddled his horse, vaguely aware that someone was calling to him. When he tightened the cinch, the voice grew more insistent, and he turned to see Ginny Settle climbing over the split-rail fence into the corral.

"What is it? What's wrong? Daddy won't tell me. What happened to Red?" she asked.

"Apaches. They have a work crew pinned down over by Black Mesa."

Ginny raised a hand to her mouth, as if to suppress a cry, but her voice was calm when she lowered it. "Slocum, why is this happening? What's going on around here?"

"I wish to Christ I knew," he said. He swung up into the saddle and spurred his horse, taking the fence at a full gallop. Over his shoulder, he shouted, "Tell your father to meet me at Black Mesa. And tell him to hurry!"

She watched him ride off, then turned as the front door of the main house banged open. Vernon was buckling on his gunbelt as he sprinted to the corral. Ginny ran to the gate and opened it, and Vernon ran inside without a word.

"Daddy," she said, grabbing at his sleeve as he rushed past. "Daddy, what's—"

"Not now, Ginny. Not now. You got to take care of Red. Where's Slocum?"

"He already left. He said to meet him at Black Mesa."

Vernon busied himself with his mount, grunting as he tightened the cinch. With one foot in the stirrup, he looked at Ginny for the first time. "I like that boy," he said.

"Me too." It struck Ginny as strangely incongruous to be having such a conversation under such circumstances, and she was surprised at her own candor. Vernon looked at her hard for a moment, and she turned away. "Be careful, Daddy," she said.

"Don't worry. I'm not gonna lose this time. Tend to Red."

He goaded his horse, yipping twice as the big stallion broke into a full gallop. Far ahead, he could just make out another rider, Slocum he guessed, on the horizon, already breaking over Devil's Ridge, like a child's shaky drawing on blue paper.

Slocum glanced back, spotted Vernon far behind him, but didn't slow down. Instead, he slapped his roan's flanks, clucking to the big horse to coax the last ounce of speed from its massive shoulders. Far ahead across the flats, he could see a column of smoke. It was thick and oily looking, seeming to flow like some strange, cloudy ink. It must be the mess wagon, he thought.

Behind the column of smoke, the foothills of the Mimbres Mountains spread across his field of vision. Blurred by the already rising heat, they looked less like mountains than like an irregular smear of color across the edge of the world. The grass under his mount's hooves had been closely cropped by grazing sheep, and crisped by the sun. It hissed and crackled like invisible fire, the sound audible even over the pounding hooves.

A second column of smoke suddenly ballooned, reminding him there were two wagons with the work crew, and now it looked as if both were burning. He was still too far away to tell for certain. His heart was pounding in his ears, matching its rhythm to that of the hooves, and he breathed in huge gulps.

Slowly, the source of the fires resolved out of the blur. It was the wagons for sure. He was still too far away to see anything but dark blocks, the smoke coiling up and away like endless ropes from black boxes. The sunlight was too bright for him to see the flames, and there was no one in sight.

Pushing his horse even harder, almost recklessly, as if the animal had endless reserves of energy, he shouted, "Come on, dammit, faster, faster dammit!" The roan responded, its great head rising and falling, and flecks of foamy saliva beginning to spray back from its gasping mouth.

He could hear the gunshots now, sporadic, as if both sides were under cover. He was still too distant to see anyone, even standing in the open, and the sound was vague and indistinct. He couldn't be sure how close to the wagons Settle's men were. The towering mesa off to the left would have been an ideal place for the Apaches to take refuge after staging a hit-and-run attack.

Slocum was closing on the wagons under a full head of steam. They were starting to resolve now, and he could see that the mess wagon was already reduced to little more than a burned-out hulk. The wagon box had lost its wheels, which lay smoking on the ground. The steel hoops supporting the canvas roof had sprung loose and curled like the fingers of a skeletal hand, clawing at the blue air with black fingers.

The other wagon was still on its wheels, but it too was burned beyond salvation. He was close enough to see the flames now, and the gunshots, still sporadic, were crisp and clear in the hot morning air. Each cracked, then echoed and reechoed.

He raced past the burning wrecks, leaning forward to unboot his Winchester and scanning the flat expanse between wagons and mesa for any sign of the work crew. Lafe Hedges was supposed to be foreman, and Slocum shouted his name, but there was no answer.

Two quick shots spilled out of the air, and Slocum looked up toward the broken rim of the bluish gray mesa. He saw a tiny figure balance on a rock then leap to another. The figure was tiny, but there was no doubt it was an Apache. As he raced on, Slocum saw the Indian leap to the top of a chimney rock, balance precariously on one foot, his arms flailing, then drop to his stomach.

A moment later, the Indian lowered himself over the edge, his feet scratching at the side of the column for support. He had a rope looped around the column and worked his way down like a lumberjack. His beige blouse and the buckskin breeches and leggings blended in with the pale rock, and Slocum was able to chart his downward progress only by the thin red sliver of his headband.

Too far away to waste a shot, Slocum angled to the right as a shot cracked from ground level. He saw a spit of fire where the bullet sparked a few feet over the Apache's head, and then the Indian was down behind a jungle of smaller pillars and out of sight.

Slocum skidded to a halt a hundred yards from the mounded rubble at the foot of the mesa. Leaping from the saddle, he sprinted into the rocks, then worked his way forward until he came up behind Lafe Hedges.

"You all there is, Slocum?" Lafe asked, without taking his eyes off the spot where the Apache had vanished.

"Vernon's coming. He sent Wilson Bumpers for help, but it'll be a while. What happened? Red said you were jumped."

"Red gonna make it?"

"Not sure. He lost a lot of blood."

Lafe nodded, as if it was no more or less than he had expected. "They come on us real sudden. We was away from the wagons, running down some strays and some calves. We was spread out all to hell and gone, so they was able to pick us off easy. Juanito's dead. So is Richards. Couple more of the boys have been hit. They're back along the wall somewhere. By the time we got ourselves together to hit 'em back . . ." He shook his head.

"How many?"

"Hell, how many's it take? Five, maybe six. I don't even know for sure."

"You get any of them?"

Lafe shook his head. "Not a one. Once we got over the surprise and started to push back, they run for the mesa. They get in there, they're like termites. Got to smoke 'em out or just walk away and let 'em have the house."

"How many able-bodied men you got left?"

"Two, plus me. They're strung out along the bottom of the wall behind me."

"I'll be back."

"You keep your head down. One of them bastards is a crack shot. Dropped Juanito from two hundred yards. Right through the damn head. He never knew what hit 'im, poor little greaser."

Slocum scurried through the rocks feeling more like a chipmunk under siege than a human being. One of the Apaches spotted him and dropped two quick shots his way, narrowly missing him both times. As it was, a sliver of rock or a bullet fragment—he wasn't sure which—sliced along the back of his head just below his ear. It stung like hell as sweat dribbled into the cut, and he brought his fingers away all bloody. He clapped a hand over the wound and kept on jackrabbiting from rock to rock.

He found Tony Richards first, only Tony was going to be no help at all. He lay on his back, a bright stain on his chest already drawing flies. Slocum didn't want to turn him over. He knew the hole in back would be a lot larger. And a lot uglier.

"Anybody there?" he called, not expecting an answer.

"That you, Slocum?"

"Yeah, Billy, where are you?"

"Not where I want to be, that's for damn sure. I been hit. I think my arm's broke."

"You bleeding?"

"Pretty bad. I got it wrapped, but it won't stop."

"Hang on, I'll be there in a second."

Slocum looked at the towering wall, sweeping it with one quick glance then moving back slowly, checking it yard by yard. He got up into a crouch and started to move when a slug whined past, slamming into the dirt a few feet ahead of him. He spun back, but the shooter was already out of sight.

The Apaches held all the cards now. They could fire when they wanted and they could sit all afternoon if they felt like it. No sane man was going to try to scale the wall to get at them, and unless one of the bucks made a stupid mistake, he was in no danger whatsoever. Slocum started again, waiting in the awful eternity between one rock and another for a slug to slam into his back. But it never came.

Falling to his knees, he scrambled in among the rocks, calling for Billy LaBarge. "Billy? You still there?"

The answering voice was low, much weaker than it had been. "Where the hell would I go, Slocum?"

It came from the left, and Slocum swung around a boulder. He could see Billy's feet, jutting out from behind a canted slab. There was ten yards of open space, but he had to chance it. It sounded as if LaBarge was losing consciousness. If he lost much more blood, there would be little they could do for him.

Gritting his teeth, Slocum made a false start. Once more, a bullet ripped past him, glanced off a rock a few feet away, then whistled up and into the sky. Once more he started, and once more a rifle cracked. It seemed almost as if the Apaches were using LaBarge as bait.

But Slocum was determined they find him a tough fish to land. He started back the other way, just for a split second, enough to draw the Apache's aim, then reversed his field and broke for the tight pocket in which LaBarge lay. The maneuver was risky, and it nearly didn't work. Another shot chipped his left heel as he dove for the ground. The impact wrenched his foot to one side, and he was thankful it hadn't been a few inches to the left.

LaBarge lay on his back. The sickly sweet smell of blood filled the small pocket among the stones. A pool of blood on the ground had already started to congeal. A bloody rag, poorly knotted around the arm, trailed in the sticky sand. It had slipped down away from the ugly wound in LaBarge's arm. The cowhand had his uninjured arm draped across his eyes to shield them from the brilliant sun. His hat had tipped back and off and lay on its crown just behind his head, sitting there like a beggar's bowl. And just as empty.

"Billy," Slocum called, drawing the draped arm away. "Billy?"

LaBarge said nothing. As the arm came away, Slocum knew why. The eyes were already glazed over. They stared up at nothing, as if they were trying to look through the blue-white above them, the way a kid tries to look all the way to the bottom of a well.

Slocum reached out with one trembling hand and, with his thumb, pressed the lids closed over one dead eye, then the other.

14

"Lafe, can you hear me?"

Slocum watched the wall while he waited for an answer. When none came, he called again. "Lafe, Lafe, you all right?"

"Okay, Slocum."

"Billy's dead, Lafe."

"Jesus Christ!"

"Over here, Slocum." It was Dan Menendez. "Dougherty's with me. We're both okay."

"Anybody else?"

The silence was answer enough. And they were trapped now, unable to get clear without coming under the Apache guns. "We better join up, Dan. Dougherty, you help cover him. When he's clear, we'll cover you. Then we got to get to Lafe."

"You crazy?"

"If we wait, they'll come down. One by one, they'll get to us. If we're together, we have a chance."

"Where's Vernon?"

"He's coming, but he won't have anybody with him. He sent for help, but it'll take a while. And we won't be able to wait long enough. Lafe and I'll cover you two. Wait for my signal."

Slocum shouted the other way and when Lafe was set,

he shouted to Menendez, "Go, Dan. Move it."

All hell broke loose far up the wall. Six rifles opened up, and he could hear the slugs whistling past him toward Menendez and Dougherty. Slocum fired back, taking his time, looking for targets. But when none presented itself, he started firing into the shadowy crannies from which the cloudy puffs of gunsmoke were being spat.

Lafe was banging away from his position, and it cut the Apache fire way down, but didn't stop it. Slocum heard heavy steps as Menendez raced toward him. Dougherty, too, was firing randomly. The Apaches were cautious, and the chance of a stray bullet kept their heads down.

When Menendez tumbled into the rocks behind him, he turned. The dark-skinned Mexican lay on his stomach, breathing heavily through his mouth. Slocum could smell the fear sweat on him, filling the tight confines of the pocket. "You all right, Dan?"

Menendez nodded feebly, his nose rasping on the sandy ground because he was too exhausted, or too frightened, to raise his head. "All right, we got to cover Dougherty, now."

Menendez got to his knees. He looked at Slocum for the first time, his eyes large and bright with adrenaline. He drew his pistol and broke it open, then fumbled for bullets on the back of his gunbelt. His hands trembled and several bullets dropped to the ground. He snatched at them angrily, but when he tried to insert them into the cylinder, they kept missing. He looked at Slocum, his head shaking from side to side. He chewed at his lower lip.

"Don't worry about it, Dan. We're gonna be all right."

"I never been this scared in my life, Slocum. Never. And I was trapped by Comanches once, long time back in west Texas. I never thought I'd feel more scared than that, but . . ." He crossed himself as Slocum reached out, took the pistol and opened a palm for the bullets.

When the gun was reloaded, Slocum handed it back, then clapped Menendez on the shoulder. "Come on, now, Dan.

We got to get Dougherty over here before he thinks we don't like him anymore."

"I *don't* like him."

Slocum started to respond, when he realized Menendez was kidding. The Mexican's hands still trembled, but his eyes had shrunk to something closer to normal size. He patted the barrel of the pistol and nodded. "I'm ready," he said.

"Lafe, you set?"

"I guess . . ."

"Dougherty, go!"

Slocum opened up again. Again he was picking his shots. He heard Lafe firing as fast as he could lever shells into the chamber. Behind Slocum, Menendez emptied the revolver. Dougherty's heavy steps pounded over the sandy ground. They heard him trip and land with a sudden grunt as the air was knocked from his lungs.

One Apache, apparently realizing what was happening, or spotting Dougherty in the open, danced along the rim, momentarily upright, and Slocum was ready. He fired once, then jerked another shell home. But he didn't need it. The Indian stumbled, either because he'd been hit or because he lost his footing in trying to dodge Slocum's bullet. He fell heavily, his body half off the rim.

Lafe saw him too, and fired twice as the Apache tried to swim back away from the edge, his arms waving in desperate, useless circles. Too much of his body weight was out over the edge and he tipped down. Slocum saw the legs sawing helplessly, and then the long, slow plummet as the Indian bounced once thirty feet below the mesa's top, glanced off a chimney and veered to the right. He turned once in the air, his feet pointed down for a second, but gravity pulled him headfirst again and then he was gone.

Lafe gave a rebel yell, and the piercing shriek echoed off the suddenly silent stone, dying away slowly until everything was silent again. "That's one," Menendez said.

"Plenty more where he came from," Slocum warned.

"Plenty more goin' where he went, too," Dougherty gasped.

"Look," Slocum snapped. "We got our hands full just getting out of this alive. You get cocky, you'll get yourself killed, and maybe us right along with you."

Slocum crawled to the back edge of the pocket and looked out across the flatlands. He could see a small cloud kicked up by a solitary rider galloping toward them, probably Vernon. He snaked around and crept back, careful not to expose himself. The high ground held by the Apaches reduced them to a waiting game. If they all came down, they would give up their advantage. So there was always the chance one of the bucks might decide to come down off the mesa. If he could drive Slocum's men into the open, they'd be sitting ducks.

But if they decided to sit tight, it would keep Settle's men pinned down. And going up after them was a mistake Slocum wasn't about to make.

"What now?" Dougherty asked.

"Lafe's got better cover. We'll go over one at a time."

"You crazy? We're okay here. Let's wait it out."

"If we're all together, we stand a better chance. We can't leave Lafe out there alone."

"They won't come down. He'll be all right."

"And if they do?"

"They won't, I said."

"They're not fools. They know Red got out, they know I came and they can see Vernon right now. That means they know more help is on the way. They don't want to wait here long enough to be surrounded."

"I got an idea, Slocum. Since you seem to know so much about these red bastards, why don't you go up and talk to them? Tell them we're just going home and they should do the same."

Menendez shook his head. "Dougherty, sometimes you sound like a fool. You'd be better off keeping your mouth shut."

"Want to make me, greaser?"

"Cut it out," Slocum snapped. "We got enough trouble without fighting among ourselves."

"Who died and left you in charge, Slocum?" Dougherty snarled.

Slocum ignored him. Tapping Menendez on the shoulder, he said, "You go first, Dan. Lafe and I will cover you. We'll let Dougherty do what he wants."

Menendez smiled. "Whenever you're ready."

Slocum nodded. "Lafe, Menendez is coming over. You ready?"

"I'm almost out of ammunition, Slocum. I can't give him much cover."

"Pick your spots."

"You got it."

"Now!" Slocum popped up and fired twice at the mesa wall. He dropped to the ground, expecting a hail of bullets, but nothing happened.

He heard Lafe fire twice as Menendez scrambled across the open ground to the next cover. Still no return fire from the Apaches. What the hell's going on, he wondered.

"Look's like you scared them off, Slocum," Dougherty laughed.

"Shut up!" He peered out cautiously, scanning the wall. One by one, he picked out the small crevices where the Apaches had been, sighting down the barrel of his Winchester. There was no sign of activity. And no return fire, even when he slammed another shot into a narrow slot between two chimneys, a place from which particularly heavy fire had been coming.

Menendez shouted that he was clear. Slocum turned to Dougherty. "You going next, or are you staying here?"

Dougherty didn't answer at once. He seemed to be considering his options. Then, deciding he didn't particularly want to be on his own, he nodded. "I'm going," he grumbled, getting into a crouch and easing in behind Slocum.

"Dougherty's coming," Slocum shouted. He felt the pressure of Dougherty's body on his back increase as the surly hand pushed off with one hand on Slocum's shoulder, then he was gone.

Slocum watched the wall again. And again he saw nothing. The only noise was that of Dougherty's boots scraping on the sand. He looked back into the flats. The cloud was closer, but Settle was still a couple of miles away.

"Here I come," he shouted, breaking into a sprint. He slipped in between two large rocks, cut left, then right and dove into the jumble of boulders where Lafe and the others had their guns trained on the wall.

Lafe was shaking his head. "I can't figure it," he whispered. "It don't make no sense. Where'd they go?"

"Like I said," Dougherty laughed, "Slocum scared them off all by hisself."

Lafe glared at him but said nothing.

"You know what I think," Menendez said. "I think they're waiting for us to move again. If we think they're gone, we'll move back and when we're too far from cover, they'll chew us to pieces."

"I don't think so," Slocum said.

"Then where are they?"

"Your guess is as good as mine."

"I'll tell you one thing," Menendez said. "I ain't going out in the open before dark."

Slocum looked back over the flats. Vernon was still coming on, but it looked like his presence would make no difference. Still, they couldn't afford to take a chance. "We got to cover Vernon," Slocum said. "Watch the wall. You see anything move, I don't care what you think it is, you cut loose."

"You're wasting your time, Slocum. Those Apaches are gone, I tell you." Dougherty sounded almost angry about it, now that the threat seemed to have disappeared.

Slocum glared at him, and he mumbled something, but turned his attention to the wall looming above them.

It was a tense five minutes until Vernon Settle rode up.

"The hell you all sitting on your butts, for?" he asked, as he climbed down from his horse.

"They're gone, Vern," Lafe said. "Clean got away. But we paid a heavy price."

"What do you mean?" He looked at Slocum for the answer.

"What he means, Vernon, is that we are the survivors. The others are all dead."

"What? Jesus Christ, Slocum, you can't be serious!"

When Slocum didn't say anything, Settle turned his back. He looked away for a long time, shaking his head once in a while and looking at the sky as if it could explain what had happened. Finally, letting out a long shuddering sigh, Settle turned back. He raised one tanned fist to his cheek for a second, wiping at something without comment. He looked at the tip of his finger, then wiped the moisture on his shirt.

"Let's bury 'em," he said.

15

Vernon Settle climbed into the saddle and reached down for Ginny's hand. "You listen to Slocum," he said, enfolding Ginny's delicate fingers in his own massive fist. He patted the back of her hand, then leaned over to plant a kiss on the top of her head. "He's in charge while I'm away. I showed him the root cellar and the tunnel to the barn. You pay attention. He tells you to jump, you better jump."

Turning to Slocum, he said, "I wish to hell I could take you with me. But I think it's more important that you stay here. Ginny's all I got, and I'm holding you responsible for her safety."

"Mr. Settle, I think—"

"Slocum," Settle interrupted, "you hold in your hands everything I hold dear. I think maybe you could call me Vernon. I already told you that, once. Hell, men who don't have half your sense, and who I respect a lot less, call me Vernon. You might just as well."

Slocum nodded. "All right, then, Vernon. I think maybe you ought to reconsider. This is getting way out of hand now. Rumors about other Apaches leaving the reservation are thick as leaves. I think maybe it's beyond anybody but the Army, now."

"Son, them Apaches have been running on and off the reservation as long I can remember. The trouble is, the

98

Army lets them surrender. They take the savages back to San Carlos or Fort Apache and turn 'em loose. The next thing you know they're right back on the warpath. No sir, this is not a job for the Army. This is a job for men who know there's only one solution, an end to it, once and for all. We got near a hundred and fifty men and we're gonna do it right, this time. I'll be back in two, maybe three weeks. No longer than that. In the meantime . . . well, you know what to do."

Settle stretched to his full height and looked out toward the mountains, where tiny figures were dribbling in from every direction. It was an awesome force, but Slocum wasn't convinced it would make any difference. These were men who were fueled by anger, by hatred and by frustration. Some of them hadn't even been directly affected by the latest Apache depredations. But there was a kind of manic party atmosphere infecting the whole territory. It was beyond one man's stopping.

Slocum knew that it could end badly, and not just for the Apaches, but he'd tried several times in the last week to convince Vernon Settle that it wouldn't work. When they buried Billy LaBarge and Tony and Juanito, and the others, Vernon had stood quietly by the graves. He wasn't listening to Slocum then, and he wasn't listening to Slocum now. He had his mind made up.

They watched him turn his horse and trot out of the yard. Ginny wiped at her cheek once or twice, but Slocum couldn't tell whether it was to brush away a tear or if it was just out of nervousness. In the long run, though, there would be more than enough tears to go around. He knew that as surely as he knew anything. Ginny's hand sought his, the delicate fingers closing over his rough hand and squeezing it several times. He looked down at her, and she smiled.

"I guess you'd rather be going with Daddy," she said.

"No, ma'am, I wouldn't."

"You really think it's that dangerous?"

"Anytime you get a hundred and fifty angry men together, every one of them packing a gun or two, somebody's bound to get hurt. More often than not, it isn't who they set out to hurt, either." Slocum looked after Vernon's figure, now nearly as tiny as the others. The roiling dust kicked up by the horses and supply wagons stretched for miles in every direction. It was too dry by half, and Slocum couldn't remember the last time it had rained. That seemed somehow ominous, as if the world were being turned to tinder, just waiting for a spark.

And that spark wouldn't be long in coming.

"Daddy told you he wants you to stay in the big house, didn't he?" Ginny asked. She gave him a brilliant smile, more than a little coy, and Slocum nodded.

"Yeah, he told me."

"You will, won't you?"

"I guess."

"Good." She smiled again and walked toward the house. With one foot on the steps, she turned and looked over her shoulder. "You coming in?" she asked.

"Not now. I got something to tend to."

"Don't be long. I don't like being alone in this big old house."

Slocum watched her climb the steps and cross the porch, still looking back at him, until the screen door closed behind her.

He had a lot to do. During the last week, once Vernon had announced his plans, Slocum had been busy planning his defenses. Unlike Vernon, who thought the Apaches would cut and run ahead of the tide of angry ranchers, he believed the Apaches were more likely to stay in the area. The ranches would be stripped of half their men, in some cases more, and they'd be vulnerable. Once he realized Vernon couldn't be talked out of joining the assault force, he'd been studying the layout of the Settle spread.

Like most of the ranches in the area, it was wide open on every side. There was very little in the way of natural defenses, and he'd been forced to improvise. Pillboxes of raw timber, one for each point of the compass, had been erected. They were to be manned day and night, one man each during the daylight hours, and one each of the less-seasoned hands at night, when an attack was less likely.

It left more than a little to be desired, but he had to play the cards he'd been dealt. He didn't like the odds. He was forced to count on men who had nothing to gain, in a fight against men who had nothing to lose. The edge clearly went to the Apaches.

He saddled his horse and rode out to the first small barricade. Each had ammunition and a pair of binoculars. He had only eight men, so they'd all be working twelve-hour shifts. And he knew, as many of the younger men did not, that staying on the defensive had a way of sucking the life out of you. Every bird cry, every scurrying rodent, every passing shadow had to be checked. And every time you found nothing, you were less likely to pay attention to the next. Nobody knew that better than the Apaches.

Lafe Hedges was in the bunker, along with a skinny kid from Kansas named Peterson. Lafe turned as Slocum dismounted. He was leaning on the front wall, his elbows propped on the rough logs, a battered pair of binoculars sitting beside his left arm.

"Been watching them crazy boys," Lafe laughed. "Seems like a fool's errand, to me, Slocum."

Slocum agreed, but didn't want to say so. Not to the men. He was already sure he'd have his hands full. Sniping at Vernon behind his back wouldn't make his job any easier.

"Today should be pretty quiet," Slocum said. "If anything's going to happen, I figure it'll be after the main party is gone. Day after tomorrow, maybe, or the day after that. But we've got three weeks of this, so we might as well get used to it."

Lafe shook his head. "I'll bet they never fire a shot. Those Apaches'll be all the way to the Sierra Madres by now."

"I hope so. You know what to do, Lafe, right?"

Lafe nodded. "Not so sure about the scarecrow, here, though." He nudged Peterson with an elbow, and the kid grinned in embarrassment. "But I'll whip him into shape by the time the first redskin shows up. Nothing to worry about on this end."

To Peterson, Slocum said, "You ought to go to the bunkhouse and get some sleep. You'll need to be wide awake for your night shift."

"I tried, but I can't sleep, Mr. Slocum."

"Try again."

Slocum walked back to his horse and swung into the saddle. "I'll be by later, to see how it's going."

"I'll tell you one thing, Slocum. This sure as hell beats workin'," Lafe shouted.

Slocum laughed. "Let's hope it stays that way."

He checked each of the battle stations in turn. Generally, the men were skeptical, in a good-natured way. He didn't blame them for their skepticism, but he couldn't afford to let them know it. Because somewhere in the back of his mind was the conviction not only that the precautions might come in handy, but the fear that they might not be enough.

Back at the house, he sat on the porch, looking at the thinning dust cloud. The war party was long since out of sight. It was quiet. Almost too quiet, he thought. Restless, he got up and went inside to check on Ginny.

She was sitting at the piano in the large, sunlit living room, sheet music open on her lap. She looked up when he entered. A large grandfather clock in one corner started to toll, filling the room with its sonorous chimes. Ginny glanced at it, then smiled at him. "Ten o'clock, and all's well," she laughed.

Slocum smiled in spite of himself. She was even prettier than he'd realized. There was something lively about her in the past few days, as if some cloud had been lifted, letting her full radiance shine forth.

"You like Beethoven, Mr. Slocum?"

"I'm not much for music, Miss Settle. My mama used to play the piano, but it's been a long, long time."

"Would you like to hear me play?"

"Sure, why not."

He lowered himself into a large, overstuffed easy chair, but Ginny frowned. Patting the piano bench, she said, "Sit here."

"I can hear all right from right where I am," he said.

She pouted, and he laughed. "All right, all right."

"I don't bite, you know." She waited for him to sit beside her, then stuck out her tongue. "At least, not lately."

She smoothed the music and placed it on the music stand above the keyboard. "This is one of my favorite pieces," she said. " 'The Moonlight Sonata.' Do you know it?"

"Not well, but I've heard it."

She poised her hands over the keys, cocked her head coquettishly for a second, then began to play. The complex chords posed no difficulty, and the music filled the room. Absorbed in the music, she paid him no mind. He had the feeling that she had forgotten he was there.

She never stumbled, even over the more difficult passages, and her rhythm was nearly flawless. She took some sections at a breakneck pace, the waves of sound as consistent and powerful as breakers right after a storm. His mother had played the piece often, and he remembered more of it than he would have thought.

But Ginny's approach was more tempestuous than his mother's had been. Instead of reflective, it was aggressive, as if Ginny found the quiet passages too tame for something boiling up inside her. After twenty minutes, she neared the end, racing now, picking up the tempo as if she were in a desperate race. Then, the last chords struck, she pedaled and let them fade away, her hands in her lap.

Only when the music had died did she look at him again.

"Did you like it?" she asked. Her brows were knit as if she were waiting for a critic's opinion and her career depended on the review.

He nodded, and she smiled again. "I'm glad." She rested one hand on his thigh, and he felt a little twitch of nervousness. He stood up hurriedly.

"Where are you going?" she asked.

"Want to check the corral, make sure the horses have been fed."

"I fed them myself, this morning."

"Just want to make sure."

"Don't you trust me, Mr. Slocum?"

She looked hard at him, something aggressive barely hidden behind the broad smile.

He didn't answer.

16

There had been two false alarms already. The men were edgy, and Slocum didn't blame them. Far better to get excited about nothing than to ignore something that was really there. Lighting a cigarette, he stood on the porch watching the sun sink in the west. The saw-toothed mountains scratched away at the flattened ball, trying to cut it in half, but it sat there, balanced on the highest peaks, hung up like a kite on a tree limb.

The smoke calmed him a little, but his nerves were fraying at the edges, ready to snap at the first serious pull. He sucked at the tobacco, filling his lungs with the smoke three or four times, then coughed out the last of it and flicked the butt away. He watched it land a few feet from the porch, then realized he'd better tell the men not to smoke on his next tour of the defenses.

He walked to the barn and looked back at the house for a few moments before going inside. Already, Ginny had a lamp burning in her bedroom on the second floor. The windows were picking up orange light from the sun, and the glow of her lamp was only visible if he cocked his head to one side to avoid the glare.

He hadn't seen her since the afternoon. Maybe she's getting the point, he thought. But he doubted it. In the barn, he climbed to the loft and then to the ladder which took him up through a hatch onto the roof. The binoculars draped around his neck seemed to weigh a ton, but he knew it was not the glasses but the reason he wore them at all that pressed so heavily down on him.

This was his last chance to pick up anything by daylight, and he worked the glasses methodically scanning out to the horizon then back in, then out again, strip by strip examining the desolate flatlands that surrounded the Settle spread. There was little to see, and nothing but a few stray tumbleweeds moved across his line of sight. If the Apaches were out there, he had no doubt they'd be paying a visit. But he didn't know, and it was the not knowing that had done such a job on him.

The sun was getting redder, and he wanted to make his last circuit of the night before it got too dark. Letting the glasses fall against his chest, he climbed back through the roof hatch and worked his way down the ladder. Once on the ground again, he moved quickly, taking his horse from the corral and mounting in a single fluid motion.

Ginny's curtains were pulled aside now, and he thought he saw her moving behind the glass. He rode to the bunkhouse, where the night sentries were waiting on the porch, whispering among themselves.

They were kids, mostly, little more than schoolboys, and they were scared. All the emphasis on security had them spooked, and they wanted reassurance. But Slocum had none to give them.

One of the kids, a local boy named Roger Harmon, was practicing a quick draw, even while he chatted with the other three. He nodded when Slocum rode up, but kept on slapping his hip. Twice, his Colt fell to the ground, and the other three ragged him, but he kept at it.

"You fixin' to draw down on somebody, Roger?" Slocum asked, provoking giggles from the others.

"No harm in being ready, Mr. Slocum."

"You're right, Roger. No harm. But I've got to tell you,

Apaches don't usually call you out of a bar and ask you to go for it."

"No, sir."

"But if it makes you feel better, you keep right on practicing."

"Yes, sir."

Slocum stared at the others to forestall another round of giggles.

"Time to go, fellas. You all get some shut-eye this afternoon, like I told you?"

"Hard to sleep in daylight, Mr. Slocum," Harmon said.

"Well, just make sure you stay awake tonight."

Harmon nodded.

"You boys go on out and take your posts, now. I'll be along in a bit."

He watched them go. They kept looking back over their shoulders, as if in hopes that he was only joking. Slocum didn't like using them this way, but there was a much smaller chance of a night raid, so he was actually exposing them to the smaller risk. It was cold comfort, but it was the only comfort to be had.

On the rounds, he stopped at each of the four outposts to make sure there was plenty of ammunition and water. Other than that, the only thing he could do was cross his fingers and keep them crossed. He warned each of the men in turn that smoking at night was an invitation to a bullet, and they understood, although grudgingly, and promised not to strike a match or light a fire, either.

When he returned to the house, he saw the light still on in Ginny's window. It was dusk now, and the sky was that purple-black mass of clouds against a blue-gray background that ordinarily was so soothing. But not tonight.

He watched the last few blades of sunlight spear out from behind the clouds, turning their edges bright yellow for a minute or two, and then it was dark.

There was no moon, and wouldn't be for a few hours. He went inside and made sure the door to the root cellar would open easily. Going below, he checked the water and supplies. Everything was in order, and he climbed out of the cellar, closed the hatch, and pushed the rag rug back in place.

He thought about going up to check on Ginny, but decided he had enough to think about without any more of her teasing.

Out on the porch, he watched the night for an hour or so, wishing he could read or, better yet, sleep. But he knew there was little chance of that. It was starting to get chilly, and he went back inside. He was planning to sleep on the living room floor, but the blankets he had folded and left beside the fireplace were gone. Automatically, he looked up at the ceiling, as if he could see through into the rooms above, imagining Ginny laughing at him.

He climbed the stairs slowly. He was in no mood for any practical jokes. The door to her room was closed, but a crack of light slanted out from underneath it. She was probably still awake. He rapped on the door and got no answer but the rustle of cloth. Knocking again, he called, "Ginny? You awake?"

Still there was no answer. He was just turning to go back downstairs when he heard the doorknob turn. The door swung open, spilling light and a hint of perfume into the hall.

"It took you long enough," she said, poking her head out into the hall.

"Long enough for what?"

"To come see me."

"I didn't come here for that. I came to find out what happened to my bedroll."

"It's in here, Mr. Slocum," she said.

Sighing in annoyance, he shook his head and stepped up to the door. With one hand extended, he said, "Can I have the blankets, please, Ginny?"

"It's 'may,' Mr. Slocum, and no, you can't."

"Why not?"

"Because I think you should stay up here. I'm frightened in this big old house."

He stepped into the room. "Frightened of what?"

"I don't know." She was wearing a flannel nightgown that had all the allure of a cotton sack. But there was something about her that made the gown irrelevant. While he waited, she went to the window and tugged the curtains closed, then the heavier drapes.

She pointed to the bedroll on the floor alongside the bed. "You can sleep there," she said, cracking a smile that showed no hint of the fear she claimed to feel. "Close the door."

When he didn't, she stepped past him, making no attempt to conceal her annoyance. The door banged shut and she turned the key in the lock then tossed it onto the bed. Walking back to the bed, she circled around it and lowered the lampwick until the room was barely lit.

Then, so fast he wasn't sure it happened, she bent, grabbed the hem of the gown and swished it up and off. She turned away for a moment, tossed the gown into a corner, then turned back, her hands on her hips.

"What do you think?" she asked, pirouetting. Her hair spilled down her back nearly to her ass, and a very solid ass it was, Slocum noticed.

"About what?" he asked.

"What do you think?" Her voice was husky now, as she walked toward him, skirting the bed without averting her eyes. Her breasts bobbed with the movement, the broad hips, accented by her tiny waist, rolled seductively.   •

He was aware of the thick triangle of hair catching the light and looking almost like bronze. He stood motionless, thinking she was just teasing him again, brazenly, but almost certainly with a limit to how far she would go. He made a move to leave, but she had locked the door. And then he realized he didn't really want to leave anyway.

As the thought flitted in and out of his consciousness, Ginny smiled, as if she'd read his mind. She got to him and he was aware of his back pressing against the door. She stood and tiptoed, closed her eyes and leaned up with puckered lips. He brushed his lips against her, but her mouth opened and her tongue darted into his surprised gasp like liquid fire.

In spite of his uncertainty, he let his hands settle on her hips then slide down to pull her closer, his palms against the smooth, cool flesh of her magnificent ass. He felt the hardness of her nipples pressing against him, even through his clothes. He was aware that he hadn't had a bath, and aware, too, that it didn't seem to bother Ginny. He felt her fingers working at his gunbelt as he continued to stroke her from shoulders to thighs, his rough hands gliding over the silken skin as if it had been oiled.

His shirt was open and she tugged his pants down, then knelt to pull off his boots. She was confident now that he wasn't going anywhere. He stepped out of his pants and she straightened, taking him by the hand and pulling him toward the bed. Suddenly, she pivoted and shoved him backward. The backs of his knees caught the edge of the bed and he fell.

Straddling him, she leaned forward, lowering her breasts over his open mouth, then reached out with one hand to cup one breast and press it against his flicking tongue. He sucked greedily, changed to the second breast, then back. He felt himself growing hard, and Ginny sensed it too. She reached back and took him in her hand, stroking firmly, wriggling her ass back against the length of him. He continued to suck at her breasts, and she let a low moan escape as she hoisted her hips and guided him home.

He felt the head of his cock suddenly enveloped. Then, with a powerful thrust, she lowered herself on him full length, throwing her head back and groaning. He started to move, slowly at first, then faster as her hips rose and fell. His hands slid along her ribs, then up, each taking a full breast, and he worked his thumbs against her nipples as she started to twitch her hips from side to side, almost raising herself up and off, pausing at full height, then plunging down again.

He heard the thick sucking sounds of their sweaty skins, and it seemed to make her move faster and faster, even as he jacked his hips higher and higher on every thrust. He trembled now, trying to hold back but unable to resist the persuasive heat of her, the demanding ripple of muscles in her vagina as they goaded him to a climax he could not refuse.

She moaned again, pressing herself down further and further, harder and harder, as if she sought to crush him, then screeched, gave a sharp gasp ending in a husky sigh, and fell forward, draping her flesh over him and breathing hotly in his ear.

"Don't even think of sleeping tonight, Mr. Slocum," she whispered. "We're just getting started." As if to tease him again, she wiggled her hips and he felt his erection quiver as she pulled away for a moment, then settled her body against him once more.

17

Slocum was up early. He looked at Ginny, still sleeping, the blanket down around her waist. She really had an extraordinary body, he thought. And energy to match. For a moment, he found himself wondering what Vernon would say if he were to find out. But the more he thought about it, the less he worried. Vernon would probably not be in the least surprised; but he wouldn't like it, either. That was a certainty.

What Ginny herself would think was another matter. She had taken advantage of him, and he of her. But that sounded almost like an excuse for a roll in the hay. It probably was, he thought, then caught himself grinning in the mirror of her vanity.

He dressed quietly, then went downstairs to the porch. He wondered why he didn't feel bad about what happened the night before. He tossed the idea around for a half hour before deciding there was no reason he should. By sunrise, he'd come to grips with the irreversible fact.

He was on the porch when Ginny came out with a mug of coffee for him. "Sleep well?" she asked.

"Eventually."

"I watched you for a while. I've never done that before, you know? Spent the night with a man, I mean. I wasn't a virgin, but I guess you could tell that."

Slocum nodded. "That wasn't quite fair, you know, Miss Settle."

"You can get even whenever you want." She stuck her tongue out and screwed her features into an impish grin.

"I don't think so."

"But I promise, I won't mind . . ." She kept the coffee just out of his reach, teasing him with it the same way she had teased him with her body. Finally, sensing that he was in no mood, she brought it close enough for him to take it, then closed the fingers of her free hand over his. "I'm not sorry, you know. And you shouldn't be either."

"I'm not."

"Good." She tossed her hair, still down but brushed into long waves of copper. "We made it through the night. I guess maybe you were worried about nothing. The Apaches, I mean."

"There's plenty of time. One day doesn't mean anything. Besides, if they come, it will be during daylight. They like to see what they're doing."

"They won't bother us. I think Daddy's right. They're running for Mexico."

"I hope so."

He sipped the coffee, unwilling to prolong the conversation. He needed time to think. Without her body to distract him, he needed to think about defending the ranch, and to think about his future on it. It seemed clear he'd have to move on, now. Settle, whatever he might really believe, would probably feel compelled to kill him if he ever learned what happened. Honor required things like that, and Vernon Settle seemed to be a man addicted to honor. And if Ginny's current behavior were an indication, there was no way in hell he wouldn't.

Ginny sat on the top step of the porch. There was a coil of smoke in the bunkhouse chimney, and she watched it curl lazily upward. Slocum watched her in profile. She really was beautiful, he thought. He shook his head, and Ginny must have heard the rustle of clothing. She turned and he expected her to smile. But she didn't.

"Anything wrong?" he asked.

"I'm worried about my father, that's all. He's too old to be running around the mountains chasing after Indians."

"He's got a lot of life in him yet, Miss Settle. He'll be all right, as long as he doesn't do anything foolish."

"But he already has. Isn't that what you think?" She watched him closely, as if she expected his face to contradict his words.

"Yes, that's what I think. But I've been wrong before. Lots of times."

"And this time?"

"I don't know." He drained the rest of the coffee in a long gulp, ignoring the searing heat, then set the mug on the porch floor. Getting to his feet, he moved to the steps and looked out across the flatlands. It was so peaceful, it was hard to believe there were men out there willing to skin a man alive or gut him like a trout and leave him to die a slow and horrible death.

But those men *were* out there, and he couldn't afford to let the superficial quiet of an early summer morning lull him into forgetting it. "Twenty days," he whispered. "That's all, just twenty days more."

"Did you say something?" Ginny asked. She stood and wrapped an arm around his waist, but he pulled away. She seemed hurt. "I don't care if someone sees," she said.

"But I do."

She laughed, then. "Big strong man like you, Mr. Slocum," she was mocking him now, affecting a thick Southern drawl that surpassed his own, "I declare, I wouldn't think you'd be afraid of *any*thang."

He laughed in spite of himself. "You're a cruel woman, Miss Settle," he said. "But I think I—"

The gunshot stopped him. He took her by the shoulder roughly, and pushed her toward the door. "Get inside!"

"But it's probably nothing. One of the boys just—"

"Inside, *now!*" He yanked open the door and gave her

a shove, more roughly than he'd intended. She stumbled inside and pulled the heavy main door closed.

Men were already spilling out of the bunkhouse, some of them only half-dressed. Lafe, in his pants and long-johns shirt, gunbelt looped over one shoulder, raced toward him. "The hell was that?" he asked. A second gunshot, then a sharp burst of three or four answered before Slocum could say a thing.

"That's over by Harmon," Slocum said. "Come on . . ."

He ran to the corral and tugged his horse, already saddled, out of the open gate. Swinging into the saddle, he shouted, "Lafe, leave Dougherty at the house, then get over to Harmon's post."

Lafe was already sprinting back to the bunkhouse, barking orders at the top of his lungs. Slocum rounded the barn, and could see already that they were in deep trouble. Somebody, almost certainly Harmon, lay draped over the barricade. Even at this distance, Slocum could see the dark red stain on the back of Harmon's shirt.

It was too late to help the kid, and he turned his attention to another barricade. Two gunshots, both from a long gun, cracked as he spun his mount. He saw Randolph Hassey running toward him, and behind Hassey, on foot, were two Apaches.

Slocum charged forward, trying to draw a bead on the bucks, but Hassey was weaving from side to side, and the Apaches were right behind him. There just wasn't any margin for error. On horseback, he was closing the gap quickly, and he shouted for Hassey to turn aside.

The young hand looked at him, his eyes big as saucers, and tried to turn, but he stumbled. Slocum fired twice, the Colt Navy bucking against his thumb. One of the Apaches fell, but the second was closing the gap so quickly, he was on Hassey before Slocum could fire.

Hassey fell, and the buck scrambled onto his back. He had a long knife, and as he raised it high over his head, Slocum snapped off a shot, missed, and fired again as the knife began its long, downward arc. The bullet slammed into the buck high on the shoulder. Slocum heard bone break and saw the knife come all the way down, even as the Apache fell to one side.

Hassey screamed, then started to scramble out from under the Indian's dead weight. Slocum dismounted and raced to the kid, bending to drag the dead Apache off Hassey's flailing legs. With the weight off him, Hassey scrambled away, still screaming. He started to run, and Slocum had to tackle him.

The kid started to cry now, and Slocum saw the long gash on his arm, where the blade had sliced along the biceps and cut the shirtsleeve. Blood was pouring down the arm, dripping from the fingers, even with Hassey's other hand clasped over the ugly wound.

"Come on, Randolph, we got to get that arm looked after."

"Sonofabitch, sonofabitch," Hassey snuffled. "Sonofabitch." He sniffed, then looked at Slocum. "He would'a' killed me, you hadn't been there, Slocum."

"You don't get a move on, one of his friends surely will."

Hassey nodded. "I know, I know that, I know it."

"Can you walk?"

The kid shook his head. "Yeah, I can walk. Feel dizzy, though."

"That's the bleeding. You get to the house and lie down. Miss Settle'll bandage that gash for you. Can you make it that far?"

Hassey started walking. "If not, I'll be somewhere between here and there," he said, trying to laugh.

Slocum remounted and headed toward the next outpost. Lafe and the others were already on the way, racing on foot. A puff of smoke appeared over the bunkhouse, and for a moment, Slocum thought it was just the last gasp of the breakfast fire. But the smoke started to thicken, and he realized the Apaches had set the building on fire.

He shouted to Lafe, but his yell was drowned out by a

sudden fusillade. Plumes of gunsmoke sprouted like weeds in the middle of the charging knot of men. An Apache appeared at the far end of the bunkhouse, a torch in one hand, a revolver in the other. The Indian hadn't seen him, and Slocum skidded to a halt. Yanking his Winchester clear, he aimed and fired, then levered a second shell home as the Indian fell to one knee.

The torch lay on the ground, up against the wall of the bunkhouse, and the dry wood was certain to catch unless he could get there in time. The Apache pivoted, looking around him with an expression of slack surprise. Slocum fired again, slamming the Apache back against the wall, where he slumped down, one leg bent awkwardly beneath him.

Slocum raced toward the building, jerking another shell home, and a second buck turned the corner. Slocum was still fifty yards away and he fired from the hip. The bullet sent a shower of splinters flying as the Apache ducked back behind the corner of the building.

The flames were already beginning to blacken the wall where the torch lay up against the wood. As he closed on the building, one eye on the far corner, he fired again, just to keep the Apache honest. When he reached the wall, he kicked the torch aside, kicked dirt on the glowing boards at the bottom of the wall, then dashed toward the corner.

The Apache heard him coming and darted out, his revolver waist high. Slocum dove, skidded on his chest and cut loose with another shot from the Winchester. The impact had thrown his aim off and the Apache backed away, bringing his revolver down as Slocum rolled to his left, away from the wall. He heard the crack of the gun and the impact of the bullet in the dry ground just beside him.

Drawing the Colt Navy as he rolled once more, he lay on his back and fired back over his head, catching the Indian in the thigh. The Apache limped back behind the wall, and fired once more as Slocum scrambled to his feet.

The house would be next, he was certain of that. He glanced toward the porch, and saw Dougherty slumped on the stairs, his pistol just out of reach of his dead fingers.

And Ginny was inside. Alone.

18

Slocum beat at the flames on the end of the bunkhouse, trying to extinguish the blaze, but it was hopeless. He broke for the house. He stopped to check on Dougherty, but there was no doubt in his mind the man was dead. When he felt no pulse, Slocum raced up on the porch. The door was locked. "Ginny," he called. "Ginny, it's me, Slocum."

He heard the bolt slide back and then the inner door swung open. He clawed at the screen, jerked it aside, then bulled his way in, almost knocking Ginny down in the process.

"The root cellar," he said. "Come on." Racing toward the back of the house, he dragged her by the arm. Kicking aside the knotted rug, he bent to haul the trapdoor up. "Go on," he snapped, sliding the bolt again, "get down there."

She shook her head, more in confusion than outright refusal. "I don't . . . what's happening?"

"Never mind, there's no time to explain." He put his hands on her shoulders and guided her to the opening. "Watch your step."

Ginny felt for the top rung of the ladder, found it, then brought her other leg down into the opening. Slocum kept pressing her down, and she wiggled her shoulders to try to relieve the pressure. "You're hurting me," she said.

"Sorry, but you've got to hurry. There's no time to lose.

Dougherty's dead, Harmon's dead and I don't know who else. Did Hassey get here all right?"

"Hassey, no I . . . why . . . ?"

Slocum shook his head. "Never mind."

She was in the cellar to her hips now, and he knelt beside the trapdoor, pushing her down with one hand. "Come on, come on," he said.

"What are you going to do?"

"That depends. Listen to me, now. Stay down here. No matter what happens, stay down. Remember, there's a small shaft to the barn, but don't use it unless you have to. They might burn the house, so if it gets too hot, use the tunnel, but whatever you do, don't come up. Don't use the lantern. And keep the gun in your hands, no matter what. Anybody opens the trapdoor, you shoot first, understand?"

She nodded, and swallowed hard. "I'm frightened," she said. Her voice was calm. She was, so far, still able to control her fear, but Slocum knew that wouldn't last. He wished he could stay with her, but somebody had to keep the Apaches away from the house, and he didn't know if Lafe or any of the others were still alive.

"You'll be all right, as long as you do as I say. I'll come back for you as soon as the Apaches are gone."

"Suppose they—"

"They won't. Don't even think about that. They won't."

She dropped the last two rungs, and Slocum could just make out her upturned face all but swallowed by the darkness. He couldn't even see her shoulders, and her face seemed to float there in the darkness like some strange apparition at the bottom of a well.

He heard footsteps on the porch stairs and dropped the trapdoor into place, then kicked the rug back over it. The rug wasn't any real cover, but if the Apaches didn't bother to move it, they'd never know the root cellar was there. Even if they did move the rug, they might not notice the close-fitting cover. Only the bolt and a knothole which served as a finger grip enabled it to be opened.

He moved back toward the front of the house, took cover beside a doorframe and stuffed several cartridges into the Winchester's magazine. Then, cradling the carbine in the crook of one elbow, he broke the Colt Navy open, ejected the empties, and reloaded.

There was a shadowy outline against the front door's leaded glass windows. It was too vague to be identifiable, and he suppressed the urge to fire without making sure. There was no Stetson, so it almost had to be an Apache, but there was a slim chance it was not, so he waited. Someone fumbled at the lock, but the bolt was in place. With a sudden inspiration, he realized the seated bolt was a giveaway that there was someone inside the house.

On tiptoe, he approached the door, keeping low and aiming the Winchester dead center. He saw the shadow move away, covered the last few feet in two long steps, and slid the bolt open as quietly as he could.

Slocum backed away from the door as the shadowy figure appeared in a side window for a second, all but obscured by thick lace curtains. Slocum backed through the doorway toward the rear of the house. He wanted to get outside without being seen, if he could.

Flattening himself against the rear wall, he watched the window carefully. He became conscious of distant gunfire, a pitched battle from the sound of it. He concentrated on it, and realized the sound was moving, as if the men shooting at one another were racing across the flatlands to the south. For a moment, he allowed himself to hope that Lafe had rallied the remaining men and routed the Apaches.

But the more he thought about it, the less likely it seemed. If the Indians were on the run, one of them would not be skulking along the outside of the house, looking for a way in. If anything, the Apaches must be winning. It hit him like a blow in the gut, and for a second, he felt as if he couldn't breathe. He had to get out of the house. Now.

He saw nothing, no shadow, no silhouette. Nothing. Reaching for the sash, he tried to raise it. It stuck at first, then gave way with a rush. He grabbed at it in time to stop it from slamming into the top of the window frame, but the counterweights rattled in their channels, clanging against one another and drumming on the sides of their narrow chambers with the sound of a dozen drums.

When the noise died away, he reached for the lace curtains, tugged them away from the window just enough for him to look out. Once more, he heard the sound of footsteps on the front porch. Now, the door was unbolted. If the Apache tried the knob, it would turn as before but this time the door would open.

There was no time to lose. Slipping behind the lace, he peered out the window. With his hat in one hand, he looked to either side, sticking his head out just far enough to determine whether anyone was lurking along the back side of the house.

There was no one. He set the carbine down where he could reach it and he tumbled through, landed on his shoulders and rolled over. Springing to his feet, he reached back for the Winchester, propped just inside the window, then tugged the sash down. This time, it moved more easily, and he was able to lower it all the way without much noise.

Slocum looked out across the flats, toward the sound of the gunfire. It was less insistent now, as if the shooters were conserving their ammunition, or as if targets had grown suddenly scarce. The sky overhead was thickening with black smoke from the burning bunkhouse.

Moving to a corner of the back wall, he peered along the side of the house. It was deserted. To his right, there was the thin stand of cottonwoods and willows along the brook. If he could make it to the trees, he could slip along the trees and reach the back of the barn. Then, with any luck, he could watch the house, even pick off the Apache when he came out.

A solitary horse, its ancient Mexican saddle showing signs of heavy use, stood just at the corner. It trailed its reins on the ground, as if its rider planned to return soon.

Slocum heard a thump from somewhere deep inside the house, probably from the second floor. There was a crash, and then another. Glass breaking, the sound of splintering wood, one by one the sounds of pillage echoed from deep inside the Settle home. But there was nothing he could do about it now. Going inside would just expose him to the risk of being pinned down, cut off from all help, and if that happened, Ginny, too, would be helpless.

As much as the idea appalled him, he knew it was better, and safer for Ginny, if he were to stay in the open. Taking a deep breath, he broke for the trees. He steeled himself, waiting for the shout of discovery or a bullet in the back. Neither came. As he reached the trees he stumbled, and half-crawled the last ten feet until he had some cover between him and the house.

He crept into a thicket, following the course of the shallow brook that flowed down-valley, bordered by bunchgrass and tiny willows, an occasional juniper or cottonwood. He could see the house without being seen now, and he watched it quietly, like a man alone in a theater watches a performance given more for the actors' enjoyment than its solitary audience.

There was a loud crash and something, part of a chair he thought, came through an upstairs window. The window next to it burst outward, and shards of glass glinted in the smoke-dimmed sunlight as they spiraled down and shattered into still smaller pieces on the dry ground.

Then a spurt of flame licked up as the curtains were set on fire. First one, then another, and finally a third window, all in a single room, burst into flame. They went up so quickly, he was uncertain he'd seen it at all. But then puffs of smoke started belching from the glassless frames, and black soot began to cling to the walls above the windows.

The gunfire had stopped, and he tried to see past the house, out toward where he'd last seen Lafe. But there was no sign of life. The Apache was almost certain to come out the front door, and soon. Slocum moved along the tree line, trying to set himself up for a clear view of the front. He was dimly aware of his feet, dragging in the brook and filling his boots with tepid water.

Finally, he reached a spot which gave him a look at both the house and the barn. The Indian burst through the front door, ripping the screen panel from its hinges and hurling it into the yard. He kicked at the main door, breaking one window, then stalked across the porch, taking his rifle butt to the rest of the glass on the lower level of the house. One by one the windows broke, and with every new opening, more air rushed in to feed the flames already beginning to lick at the walls above the upstairs windows.

The house was beyond saving now. Slocum knew that. And yet he wanted some small satisfaction. He wanted to exact his pound of flesh, to get just a little bit closer to even, for Vernon and for Ginny. But mostly as a way of apologizing to himself for his impotence.

He heard horses approaching, and the Apache sprinted to the edge of the porch, waved a hand, then came back to the steps and started down. Slocum's rifle came up slowly. He was in no hurry. Something deep inside him told him he had all the time in the world to do what he wanted to do.

He could see the Indian now very clearly. The man's long black hair was parted neatly in the middle, held back away from his face with a dark blue headband, the face was anything but savage. It was strong-featured, and had the broad nose and striking dark eyes of his people, but had about it, too, some undeniable dignity. There was no look of murderous frenzy, but rather the determined look of a man going about his job with efficiency and a certain measure of satisfaction.

And Slocum followed him in his sights, all the way down the steps, then across the front of the house, where the Apache stood by his horse for a moment. Slocum was conscious of the pounding hooves coming closer, but he felt no sense of urgency. He had something to do and he was going to get it done. It was that simple, that matter-of-fact.

He watched the Indian move next to his horse, lean forward to snatch at the reins, then plant one foot in the short stirrups of the Mexican saddle. As he started to hoist himself up, the Indian seemed to hang suspended in space and time for a long moment.

And Slocum squeezed the trigger.

The spray of blood as the bullet found its mark seemed almost beside the point. What mattered was the look on the Apache's face. He turned halfway around, looking in vain for the face of the man who had shot him and almost certainly killed him. The Apache seemed to know that he was fatally hit.

And Slocum knew it, too.

"That's for Vernon," he whispered.

19

Slocum had no choice but to wait for nightfall. The Apaches seemed to have settled in for a long stay. By late afternoon, the house was little more than smoking ruins, and all he could do was cross his fingers and hope that Ginny had managed to get under the barn.

There had been no sign of Lafe and the others, and Slocum feared the worst. But even if they had managed to escape, they would be of little help. The horses were still in the corral, the tack along with them. Half a dozen men, if that many survived, on foot would be no match for an equal number of mounted Apaches.

What it boiled down to, after every other option had been considered and discarded, was a waiting game. Sooner or later, the Apaches would leave. There was no reason for them to stay. But there they were, as if they were waiting for something.

Or someone, Slocum suddenly thought. Maybe that was it. Maybe they were waiting to meet someone. But who?

Thin wisps of smoke continued to coil up from the ruins of the bunkhouse and the main house. The Indians were vigilant, but not overly concerned, as if they knew that Settle and his men were already far to the south, and heading toward Mexico. But how could they know that? How could they be so certain that they would be willing to wait around?

126

And Slocum came back to Rick Hardee once more. Maybe, he thought, Settle was right. Maybe Hardee had been in collusion with someone, and maybe that someone was in a position to know what Settle's plans were, just as he had known where Settle's *barranca* was, and when to hit it for the mustangs.

Turning the possibilities over and over in his head, like a man trying to figure out how to open a walnut with his fingers, Slocum kept bumping up against the stone wall he knew was there but couldn't climb—he didn't know enough, not by half. Speculation, no matter how informed it might be, was no substitute for facts.

Toward late afternoon, the Apaches grew more animated, as if an anticipated time were now fast approaching. There was a sudden creak, and the house chimney tottered, then collapsed into the ruined timbers, scattering a few sparks and sending a great cloud of ash into the air.

Slocum watched the cloud dissipate, then went back to his puzzling. The sun was already beginning to slip down behind the Mimbres Mountains when one of the Apaches shouted something and the others came running. The man who had shouted pointed with his rifle barrel at something Slocum couldn't see off to the west.

He had felt trapped all afternoon, and now he felt blind as well. Straining to see what caused the commotion, he saw only the shadowed blur of the foothills, a purple line marking the seam between the bone-dry earth and the blue sky. But something was out there, he was convinced of that. Something—or someone—the Apaches had been expecting.

And then, finally, it materialized. It was a wagon, drawn by a team of four mules. Beside it, so close as to be part of a single wavering blotch on the light background, was a man on horseback. Slocum watched the painfully slow progress, wondering who it was and whether the Apaches had known he would be coming. Was this why they had hung around? But he already knew the answer to that question. It was. It had to be.

It took half an hour for the wagon to reach the long fenced lane, rattle through the Settle gate and come to a creaking halt halfway between the barn and the ashes of the main house. The horseman was not familiar. Neither was the wagon's driver. But there now could be no doubt they had been expected.

The horseman, a tall, thin man with a ginger mustache and wisps of red hair sticking out from under his Stetson, slid from the saddle and limped to the back of the wagon. The Apaches followed him, milling like children about to get free candy from a stranger. They seemed delighted, but a little apprehensive, as if they weren't quite sure they should trust the man, but wanted to more than anything in the world.

His movement was restricted, and Slocum was forced to wait, lying motionless and cursing under his breath. He could see the Apaches, but not the tall man. The driver sat, the reins in his crooked hands, without moving or even looking around. The Apaches chattered in their guttural tongue, then one stepped aside. In his hands, he held what Slocum took to be a brand-new Winchester.

The Apache, a short man with thick thighs and long black hair draping his shoulders, pointed the new rifle at the barn, sighted carefully, lowered the rifle again to run his fingers over the gleaming metal of the barrel, then resighted. In quick succession, the warrior fired three shots, then passed the rifle to one of his tribesmen, who emptied the magazine into the barn wall. The echoes of the gunshots sounded hollow and incredibly loud. They were the only noise for several seconds.

Apparently satisfied, the Apaches each accepted a new rifle, then a crate of ammunition was taken from the wagon. The Apaches opened the crate and emptied the pasteboard boxes of shells onto the ground and proceeded to divide them. Two of the Indians went to their mounts and came back with pairs of canvas bags. The ammo was stuffed into the bags, except for six boxes. The canvas bags were returned to the horses, draped behind the saddles and lashed in place.

The remaining boxes were allocated one per buck, stuffed into pouches, and the crate's remains tossed into the ashes of the house. That quickly, it was over. The wagon made a broad turn and headed back down the lane, out through the gate and into the gathering dusk as the sound of its creaking wheels slowly dwindled. The horseman, fiddling with his mustache, conversed for a couple of minutes, then mounted and rode off after the wagon.

Slocum understood only too well what he had just seen. What he didn't understand was what it meant. Could the red-haired man be the one Settle had talked about, the man playing both ends against the middle? That he was trading in arms with the Apaches was clear, but not so clear was what they had given him in exchange for the weapons and the ammunition.

Two of the bucks, the ones who had packed the canvas bags, then went to their horses and rode off, leaving four behind. Slocum looked up at the sky, and debated launching an all-out attack. But the odds were way too long. There was no way in hell he could take all four of them, even if he managed to drop two with his first two shots. And with Ginny still huddled somewhere belowground, it was a chance he couldn't afford to take. Not if he expected to get her out alive. And that was his first concern.

All he could do was wait for nightfall. What he would do when it got dark had so far managed to elude him. But he had to do something, and soon.

When the sun was all the way down, he eased out of the undergrowth and, keeping the thicket between him and the Apaches, he circled behind the barn. The Indians were talking among themselves, partly in their own language and partly in Spanish. But the words were too indistinct for him to do anything more than identify the two tongues. As the barn shielded him from them, their voices died away to a murmur.

Now all he had to do was get into the barn without being discovered, get underground, find Ginny, get back out and get away. "Is that all?" he whispered. He shook his head at the unlikelihood. But he had no choice, and he knew it.

The sooner the better, he thought, as he started toward the back of the barn. If he could get inside, he'd have a fair chance of getting to the root cellar, or the connecting shaft, which was more than likely where Ginny was hiding. But to do that, he needed a little good luck, starting with the back door of the barn being open and its hinges reasonably quiet.

He took off his boots and tucked them out of sight and started toward the barn. He reached it quickly, and moved along the wall toward the door. When he pulled the latch string, the latch came up easily, and he eased the door partway open. The hinges started to squeal, and he held his breath. Lifting up on the outer edge of the door to take pressure off the hinges, he tried again. It came open far enough for him to slide inside.

Letting go, he pressed the door with his palm to make sure it wouldn't swing one way or the other. He thought of the wind, worried for a moment, but then decided that he couldn't spare the time, and he might have to get out a lot more quickly than he'd gotten in.

The trapdoor was in one of the stalls. He stepped in something wet and thick, cursed under his breath, and wiped his damp foot on the straw littering the floor. He found the trap, just where it was supposed to be, and knelt to grope on the floor for the rope pull. The cord was slimy, and he tugged cautiously, praying the rope hadn't rotted through. The trap popped suddenly, and he nearly fell backward, struggling to regain his balance with one hand on the floor behind him while holding onto the cord to keep the trap from slamming back down.

On an even keel again, he leaned the trap back against the wall and lowered himself into the dark hole, feeling for the ladder with his feet. He hit a rung, got a foothold, and climbed down two rungs. Looking toward the open door of the barn, he could just make out the shadows of two Apaches on the ground, wriggling where they had been cast by a newly lit fire.

Reaching back for the trap, he pulled it to him and lowered it over his head as he went down another rung. Grabbing the Winchester and pulling it down inside the hole, he went another rung, ducked his head and let the trap follow his fingertips down into the hole.

He lit a match and found the small opening on one earthen wall. It was only a couple of feet high and he had to kneel to look into it. It was pitch black, and he shook the match out and started in, after setting his hat aside.

He wanted to call out, but couldn't risk it. As his eyes grew accustomed to the gloom, he found no difference. It was absolutely black inside, not even a crack of illumination. For all he knew, he might be crawling through a blind alley toward a solid wall somewhere up ahead. After creeping on hands and knees some twenty-five or thirty feet, he struck a second match.

He heard a gasp, but could see no one. He moved the match closer to his face, trying to reassure Ginny that he was no threat. The match finally went out, and he crept forward in the dark again. Pushing the Winchester ahead with every crawling step, and careful not to jam the muzzle into the soft, damp earth of the tunnel walls, he covered another twenty feet or so. He was about to strike another match when he felt the rifle move back against his knee.

"Ginny?" he whispered.

"Slocum, thank God! I thought you were dead."

He heard scraping sounds, then felt a hand close over his knee. The fingers crept up his chest, found his face and stroked the whiskered chin. "God, I'm so scared," she said, barely suppressing a sob.

"We'll be all right," he whispered, thinking to himself just how unsure of that proposition he ought to be.

"Are they still there?"

"Four," Slocum whispered.

He hunkered around to lie on one hip, then reached out to comfort her. Instead, it provoked a bout of whimpering. She was trying to swallow her terror, but there was no way she could hold it in. "We're going to die, aren't we." It wasn't a question.

He said nothing, and she hissed at him. "Slocum, we're going to die. Aren't we?"

"Not if I can help it, Miss Settle."

He let his hand rest on her shoulder for a moment, stroking it gently, but she pulled away. "I don't believe you. There's nothing you can do to prevent it."

"Keep your voice down, dammit!" he snapped. "Even if they don't leave, they'll be asleep soon."

"But we can't get away. Can we?" There was a faint hint of hope, and he fanned it as best he could.

"Of course we can. We'll just have to be careful, and use whatever luck we have between us."

"Mine's run out," she said. "I hope you have some to spare."

So do I, Slocum thought. But he said, "Plenty."

20

Slocum went up the ladder slowly. Bracing the trapdoor with one hand, he lifted it an inch or so, listening to the sounds of the night. There was a brief scurry in the damp straw, probably a rat, and then the overwhelming silence of the cavernous barn. Raising the door another inch, and bringing his face close to the crack, he could see flickering light out through the front door. He heard no conversation. It wasn't possible to know whether the Apaches had gone or if they were sleeping. To be on the safe side, he had to assume the latter.

He raised the door further, then came up another rung, holding onto the door's edge until he was able to rest it against the wall of the stall. The rough wooden rungs of the ladder cut into his stockinged feet as he climbed the last three. He hauled himself out, leaning his rifle beside the open trapdoor.

Ginny's head appeared in the trapdoor, and she handed him her boots, which he set to one side. The muzzle of another Winchester wavered in front of him and he grasped it and set it beside the boots. He reached down to take her hand as she mounted the ladder and climbed all the way out. She wore a gunbelt that was too large for her, and had a canteen over one shoulder. Over the other, she had a canvas sack on a double drawstring, with some food and some ammunition for the two Winchesters.

He pointed to the back door, still halfway open as he had left it. She bent to reach her boots, and the canteen bumped against the wooden wall. She gasped, and then held her breath. Slocum grabbed his rifle, breathing slowly and screwing his eyes to the open door of the barn.

When nothing happened, she let her breath out slowly, grabbed the canteen in one hand and snatched at her boots with the other. On tiptoe, she moved toward the back door, and Slocum followed, walking backward and keeping his carbine leveled on the front door. He had the second Winchester in his left hand. The firelight still flickered, and he was dying to know whether the Apaches were still out there, but not willing to die in an attempt to find out.

He backed through the door, nudging it aside with one hip. Ginny was waiting, and he gestured toward the trees. She started to put her boots on, but Slocum grabbed her by the upper arm and shook his head, then pointed again to the willows. She nodded that she understood, and, with the exaggerated, birdlike stiffness of someone barefoot on rough ground, she moved away from the barn.

Slocum waited until she reached cover, then ran toward the trees, ignoring the rocks and sharp sticks poking the soles of his feet.

Ginny smiled at him. "I didn't think—" But he pressed a finger to her lips, again shaking his head. He pointed to her boots and she nodded that she understood. Sitting down, she pulled them on.

Slocum leaned close, brought his lips to her ear and whispered, "I'll be right back." He pointed to his bare feet. She nodded, and he slipped along the tree line to retrieve his boots. He was back two minutes later, sat down to pull on his boots, then stood.

Ginny leaned close, on tiptoe, and he brought his ear down for her whisper. "What now?" she asked.

Slocum pointed through the trees into the open land beyond them. She looked confused for a moment, shaping the word "Where?" with pursed lips.

Slocum shrugged. He pointed, put a finger to his lips, and watched as she moved through the trees. When she was across the brook, Slocum moved after her. The undergrowth was scanty, and he moved quickly and soundlessly to the water, crossed in two careful steps, then took her by the arm.

He didn't have a clue where they would go. But it had to be someplace close. Without horses, they wouldn't get too far during the night, and once daylight came, they'd be sitting ducks if the Apaches were still roaming around the countryside. If not, the sun would take its own toll.

They were a mile away before Ginny dared to whisper again. "What happened to Lafe, do you think?"

Slocum shook his head. "I don't know. I hope he made it out, but . . ."

She wanted to cry. He could see that. But she had some of her father's backbone, and a lot more of his enormous pride. She wouldn't give in to the impulse, and Slocum admired her for that. She might have been spoiled, pampered in an odd way, but still there was genuine courage in her.

They had to move, and Slocum took her hand. "Come on, Ginny. We can get to the Collins spread by morning. If we're lucky."

She squeezed his hand, then rushed toward him, wrapping her arms around him. "We *are* lucky, Mr. Slocum. I can feel it." She backed away a step, gave him a smile, and licked away a single tear that had trickled down her cheek. "I know it," she said.

She turned and started walking, looking back over her shoulder as if to make certain he was going to follow. It was five miles to the Collins ranch, and since Collins himself had been one of those who refused to join Vernon's hastily mounted and, to Collins's way of thinking, foolhardy campaign, there was a good chance they could get help there.

The ground was fairly level, and despite their exhaustion, they should be able to make good time. Two or three hours should do it, Slocum thought. He pulled his pocket watch to check the time. It was three A.M. They should get to the Collins spread a little after sunrise. He looked up at the black sky. The stars were so bright, they looked like pinholes in a dark canvas through which sunlight was flooding.

Slocum stopped them every mile or so, partly to let Ginny rest, without calling attention to it, and partly to go back a way to make certain they weren't being followed. It slowed them, but it was more important to get there alive than to keep to any particular timetable.

The noises of the night were subdued, as if their presence in this flat land was intimidating prey and predator alike. He found himself wondering if a ground squirrel knew when an owl was bearing down on it, or if the rat knew a rattler was on its trail. He couldn't avoid seeing himself and Ginny as helpless, despite their guns and bullets. The Apaches were past masters of this harsh country. He and Ginny, Vernon and Collins, Lafe, all of them, were interlopers, people who thought they'd conquered when they had barely learned the simple rules, and hadn't learned all the most important ones even yet. And he could only hope he would survive this latest lesson in reality.

By five-thirty, the sky was beginning to brighten. Only a handful of stars was still visible against the rising gray. And they had just over a mile to go. But as the light grew, something appeared ahead of them. Slocum felt his heart sink, but didn't want to alarm Ginny. It looked like smoke. It could just be a pocket of fog in a depression. There was no light, so if it were smoke, the fire was long since reduced to embers. But if it *were* smoke, and he could see it at that distance, he knew what it meant.

At ten to six, the sun peeked over the eastern horizon. And there was no mistaking it now. It wasn't fog. Ginny sensed something in his behavior, as if the tension had somehow sparked across the gap between them.

"What's wrong, Slocum?" Her voice cracked when she

asked the question. He shook his head, but she refused to give in that easily. "Something's wrong, I know it. What's the matter?"

He couldn't bring himself to answer. Instead, he nodded toward the Collins spread.

She looked, then turned back to him. "What? I don't see anything. What is it?"

"I'm not sure. But it looks like smoke."

Her hand went to her mouth then, as if to catch the words and force them back in. "You mean they've burned out Mr. Collins, too, don't you?"

"I don't know, Ginny. I hope to God I'm wrong. But I just don't know." He was moving faster now, and she was struggling to keep up with his longer strides. He fought the urge to break into a run, but the closer they drew, the more convinced he was that something terrible had happened. And his fear for the Collins family was slowly overwhelmed by the realization that if he was right, they had no place to turn. Collins was their best hope for help and horses.

At a half mile, he took the canvas bag from his shoulders. He groped inside for the binoculars, handed her the bag and trained the glasses on the gray pall. He'd seen the Collins home before. Not as large as Settle's place, it was still impressive.

But it was gone. He saw a single black finger, veiled in the thick smoke, pointing toward the sky. The chimney was all that remained standing. Desperately, he looked around, knowing there was no place to hide. No cover, except for the scattered trees off to the right, where a small stream wound past the Collins ranch, running behind the house and barn.

Slocum let the glasses fall. Taking Ginny by the hand, he said, "Come on, Ginny. We have to get out of the open." Moving so quickly he felt her losing her step and dragging behind him, he kept on down the gentle slope and into the thicker grass near the streambed.

He dragged her into the trees, then told her to sit. "What are you going to do, Slocum?"

"I'm going to get a better look. If the Apaches burned the place, they might still be around. The barn's still there, and there might be something we can use. You wait here until I come back. And whatever you do, don't move. I have to know exactly where you are."

She started to sob then. He knelt beside her, cupped her chin in one hand and tilted her head back. "It'll be all right. Just do what I tell you. It'll be all right."

She nodded. She didn't have the strength to do anything else, and they both knew it. Slocum stepped into the water, crossed to the far side, and broke into a trot. He had his Winchester and a pocketful of bullets, and he had the field glasses. He should be able to get close enough to see what was going on without exposing himself to anyone who might still be there.

In ten minutes, he was angling down behind the fenced-in yard. The barn appeared to be undamaged, but the house was a burned-out mound of ashes. Little wisps of smoke still curled away from some of the heavy timbers, now all charred to black slabs. A puff of wind blew past, and he saw some coals suddenly grow cherry red for a second, then fade back to gray as the wind died.

Using the glasses, he examined the yard. It was deserted, except for what appeared to be two dead bodies, one sprawled on its back near the barn, the other right in front of the house. He moved closer, ducking into a crouch and sprinting toward the back of the barn.

Pressing his back to the splintered planks of the barn side, he listened intently for nearly two minutes. He heard the soft nickering of a couple of horses, the thud of hooves, but nothing else. Moving around to the far side of the barn, he saw two horses in the corral. The fence was down, but the animals had either been left behind or had returned on their own. Neither was saddled.

Satisfied the place was deserted, Slocum stepped out from

behind the barn and circled the corral. He moved to the front of the barn and found Stan Shaw. He had been shot twice, and, for good measure, someone had slit his throat, nearly severing the head from the body. Slocum closed his eyes, fighting back the urge to vomit, and moved away from Shaw's corpse. He didn't want to look back, didn't want to think about what he'd just seen.

Approaching the remains of the house, he examined the second body. This one was Ray Collins. He, too, had been mutilated, his gut slit from breastbone to belt buckle. There were no other wounds evident, and Slocum suppressed a shudder as he thought about the slow death Collins must have suffered. The ground had been clawed by bloody hands, and smears of blood showed where Collins had tried to crawl halfway across the yard. The hands, charred to stumps, lay where the porch steps had been, as if he had been trying to get up the stairs and inside.

Slocum could think of only one reason for that.

Straightening, he looked at the burned-out ruins. Over near the chimney, he saw something, a mound of grayish white sticks, but there was still too much heat coming from the charred wreckage for him to move inside the perimeter of the house. He used the glasses again. As he brought them into focus, he saw that he had been right. Bones. Two skulls, one larger than the other. The intertwined skeletons, barely recognizable now as bones at all, must have been the remains of Ray's wife, Jenny, and their little boy.

Slocum turned away. He was halfway back to the barn before he became aware of the pain in his right hand. He looked down to see his knuckles white where he was squeezing the grip of the Winchester too tightly. The carved edges of the wooden stock were cutting into his palms. He shifted the carbine to his left hand and opened the right. There, deeply etched in the fleshy part of the palm and the soft parts of his fingers was the intricate design of the grip.

He ran into the barn, tripped over another body, a saddle beside it. He didn't recognize the man, but he had obviously been going to saddle one of the horses when he'd been caught from behind. He lay on his stomach, two bullet holes almost dead center between his shoulder blades.

Slocum grabbed the saddle and hauled it to the corral, where he saddled a big bay stallion, then went back inside for another saddle. He found a small English one on a rail and lugged it and another blanket to the second, smaller horse, a chestnut mare. Jenny Collins's horse.

Mounting the bay, he tugged the chestnut behind him and dug his heels in. He headed straight for the spot where he'd left Ginny. There was no time to waste. Getting down from the bay, he moved into the trees. "Ginny?" he called. "Come on, Ginny."

There was no answer.

21

Slocum stepped through the last of the underbrush. He called again, and still there was no answer. It couldn't be a joke. She was too upset for that, too nervous about being left alone. He moved down to the edge of the brook. Footprints, booted heels, marked the sand. As he followed them, they grew deeper and further apart, as if Ginny had started to run. Moving further along the sandy bank, he called once more. "Ginny? Where the hell are you? Answer me, dammit!" Why had she run? he wondered.

When his voice died away, all he could hear was the soft splash of the brook over the mossy stones. He saw the bag then, still fastened with its drawstring. It was lying half in the weeds and half on the sand. He ran toward it, realizing then that she was gone. Half aloud he thought, what happened here?

Reaching the bag, he bent to retrieve it. That's when he saw the second set of footprints. There were just three, firmer indentations in the sand, leading into the weeds. As his practiced eye tracked them backward, he saw where the taller weeds had been bent, the shorter grass crushed. And the prints were those of the distinctive Apache moccasin, with the curled and reinforced toe.

He felt the breath go out of him then, as if someone had landed a roundhouse to his midsection. Looping the bag over his shoulder, he followed the tracks in the grass. It was apparent now what happened. Two Apaches had come on her from the house side. She had bolted and run the other way—right into the arms of a third.

Scrutinizing the bank in both directions now he looked for the one thing he didn't want to find. After covering more than two hundred feet in either direction, he glanced up at the sky as if in thanks. There was no body. And no blood. For the moment, she was alive, but how long would that remain true?

Apaches were unpredictable when it came to prisoners, especially women. Sometimes they were virtually adopted. There were cases of women becoming the wives of Apache warriors, and one that Slocum had heard of where the woman had refused to return when she had been located.

But that was the exception.

Rape was more common, rape no less brutal than the other varieties of Apache-white intercourse. Gang rape, as often as not, the woman left battered, broken, bleeding, frequently slit from throat to crotch, laid open like a fish ready for the pan.

And for a moment Slocum wondered if it might not have been better if he had found her body in the weeds. He couldn't afford to think that way, and he tried to push the thought aside. Then something else hit him. He realized it wasn't just the potential brutality at the hands of the Apaches, it was more than that. He felt something for her. The realization confused him, and it, too, he pushed aside.

Right now he could afford to focus on one thing, and one thing only—he had to find them and get Ginny back. The rest could be dealt with later. And if he didn't get to her quickly, there would be no later.

Slocum raced to the horses, looped the canvas bag over the English saddle on the chestnut and draped the field glasses around his neck. Mounting up, he moved back along the thicker grass that followed the streambed, searching for signs of the Apaches' horses. He saw some scuff marks, evidence that Ginny was still alive, still resisting. Or so he wanted to believe.

It was nearly half a mile before he found where the horses had been left. Several horse apples, a welter of hoofprints where the animals had stood, probably hobbled, and waited for their masters. Slocum dismounted and circled the area in widening arcs until he found a trail leading away. As near as he could tell, there was a half-dozen horses. He knew for certain there were three Apaches, but there could have been as many as six. Ginny might be riding double, but he didn't think so. None of the tracks looked deep enough to have been made by a horse with a double load.

Five, then, at the most. Enough. More than enough, perhaps. Slocum remounted and used the glasses. He followed the general direction of the tracks, but there was nothing out there, nothing, however small, moving across the flats.

He nodded. "All right, then," a whisper at first, then louder, "All right. All right."

The tracks were plain, as if the Apaches didn't give a damn whether anyone followed them or not. He was thankful for that, because it meant he could make decent time. If they had been trying to disguise their trail, he would have had to take his time, stopping often to make sure he was still on their tails, and with every stop, the gap between them would have widened.

They were heading into the Mimbres Mountains. As the sun climbed higher in the sky, the temperature climbed right along with it. It was already a scorcher by ten-thirty. The world seemed to be melting before his eyes, the mountains turning to shimmering blue liquid and oozing down and across the arid plains.

The heat hammered at him, and his tongue was getting thick and pasty. He swallowed a mouthful of water, trying to conserve the limited supply in his single canteen. There would be more, in the mountains, but they were a long way away. He found himself wishing he knew the terrain better, then realized it would have meant he'd been living in hell a lot longer than he'd care to.

By noon, there was still no sign of them. Even the glasses showed him nothing. They magnified the smeary edge of the world, and the undulating waves of rising heat looked thick and slippery as glycerine as he tracked from left to right. He could pick out individual hills now, where the Mimbres started their climb, but he was still ten miles away, far enough for the molten blue to hide anything close to it.

But the Apaches were still ahead of him. And that single thing gave him hope. As long as they kept moving, Ginny would be all right. But he had to get closer, close enough that if they stopped, he could do something. But when he tried to decide what he could do, he came up with nothing.

By two, the Mimbres were resolved into distinct shapes, the blue and purple turning a more forbidding grayish blue. They were less a smeared line now, more a fence, thousands of feet high, rising up out of the plateau like an endless row of gigantic teeth. It looked almost as if he were riding into a huge mouth, one ready to chew him to pieces and spit out his bones. And that was if he were lucky.

The sun was ahead of him now, and it made it more difficult for him to see. Shielding the lenses of the binoculars, he was able to determine that the Apaches were still not within sight, but nothing else. At least now it looked as if they were planning to keep on until sundown. But the closer they got to the Mimbres Mountains, the larger loomed another specter—suppose they were returning to a rancheria? Suppose the five ahead of him were just part of a much larger band?

"What then, Johnny boy?" he whispered. "What then?"

Slocum started to second-guess himself, thinking maybe he should have let Ginny stay in the root cellar, or have brought her with him to the Collins house. But one central fact stood between him and what he might have done: he had

to do something now. Turning himself into a whipping boy
for mistakes he might have made was not going to get Ginny
back. Only he could do that, and if he allowed himself to
hang back, it wouldn't happen. Worse yet, it might get them
both killed.

He spotted a flash of light far ahead, almost on a direct
line. At first he thought it might have been a signal, but
when it wasn't repeated, he reconsidered. More likely, he
thought, it was simpler than that, a reflection from a gun
barrel, maybe. Or from Apache binoculars. If they saw him,
he'd have a much tougher row to hoe. He had no way to
know, so he decided to assume he was riding right up the
barrel of an Apache Winchester.

His water was getting low, and Slocum opened his canteen reluctantly. A mouthful was just enough to relieve the
sandpaper feeling in his throat, but nowhere near enough to
satisfy his thirst. He shook the canteen before recapping it,
and judged that he had at most two more swallows.

It was almost four-thirty when he saw another glint of
light. This time, it seemed closer. The Mimbres Mountains
were very close now, and he could see the mazelike net-
work of sloping valleys, canyons and blind alleys. The light
came from far up one of the steep cliffs, a sharp promontory
jutting up like the prow of a huge ship. As he kept his eye
on the spot, he saw it again, then a third time. This was
no signal either, he thought. But there was now the thought
that someone was looking for him, and perhaps had already
spotted him.

The trail was still fairly easy to follow, leading him to
believe that either they were leading him on or they hadn't
known that he was on their tails. But it was a whole new
card game, now. Slocum was no slouch at stud, but the
Apaches were dealing, it was their deck, and he hadn't even
had a chance to cut the cards.

As he moved into the foothills, he knew only one thing:
one mistake was all he'd get the chance to make. And if
he slipped, Ginny was gone. Whether they killed her or

kept her, Slocum was the only white man on the planet who knew where she was. If they got him, Ginny might just as well fall off the earth completely.

He had one card of his own to play. If they had seen him, they didn't know he knew it. If he could trick them into thinking he'd lost the trail, he might have a chance. It was so slim a chance he could see little possibility of it working. But it was all he had.

Checking the sun, he headed into a broad valley. He saw the trail swing off to the right. To the left, a small creek trickled down over the broken rock, and he stopped for a drink. He filled his canteen, the Apache eyes turning his spine to ice. He drank until he was afraid he'd bust his gut. Then he plunged his head underwater, tried to rinse some of the trail dust out of his hair, then straightened to let the soothing water run down over his neck and shoulders.

Back on his horse, his clothes soaked nearly to his waist, he led the chestnut into a small box canyon, where he dismounted and tied it off. He made sure there was enough grass for a day or so, and that the horse could reach the creek's sluggish current. Beyond it, there was a deep pond where the creek tumbled down off the rocks, cascading the last thirty feet in a sheet of blue-white water.

He transferred the canvas bag to his own horse. Mounting up again, he followed the creek, knowing that if he lost the trail now he might not have time to find it again. As the bay headed uphill, he could see the slanting cut of the canyon to his right. It ran off at an angle, and as he climbed, he could look down into it. He was no longer close enough to pick up traces of the Apache mounts, but if his plan was going to work, it was an inescapable risk.

The climb went slowly. His mount was picking its way carefully, and he was in no hurry now. What he wanted was sundown. If he were going to make a move, it had to be after dark. The trail flattened out a bit, and he found himself on a flat hilltop. He reined in and brought the glasses up. He scanned the trail behind him, then casually swung the glasses across the broken rock heaped beneath him. Several spots overlooked the canyon, but there was no sign of an ambush. He was starting to think he hadn't been seen after all.

Looking up, he saw the first blades of reddish light. Sundown was closing in. He dismounted now and sat with his back against a sheer wall. He used the glasses to study the terrain below. The promontory where he'd seen the light was high above him, almost dead ahead. There was a good chance the Apaches felt they'd come far enough for one day. They had been traveling hard, and they were on safe ground now, ground where the white man was at a decided disadvantage. It might be time to pitch camp.

Or so Slocum hoped.

The trails through these canyons were tricky in daylight, and only a desperate man would try to negotiate them at night. The label fit him to a T.

He watched the light change color. Slowly, it began to grow dark. Already in the shadows, it seemed to him as if the darkness in which he sat was flooding the sky, gushing upward to swallow the sun. He couldn't see a cloud, but there must have been some on the other side of the Mimbres, because the light was fragmented into broad swords of flame for a few seconds, then winked out.

And now it was time.

He thought for a moment about gathering enough wood to start a small fire. If the Apaches knew he was there and saw the fire, they would assume he'd stopped for the night. But if they took it into their heads to come after him and found the fire deserted, they'd be more alert. Better to let them think he was willing to sleep in the dark. It was unlikely they'd come looking for him in the dark. Or so he hoped.

Slocum got to his feet and grabbed the reins of the bay. He started back down the way he'd come, moving carefully to keep his footing secure. There was no way to silence the horse, but he had to have both animals near the mouth of the canyon. If he got Ginny out, and he wouldn't let himself think he might not, they were going to have to run for it.

He almost slipped once, tugged sharply on the reins and the horse started to buck. Righting himself, he stepped in close and calmed the skittish animal. When he swallowed his heart again, he started on down. Where the ride up took him a half hour, it was more than two hours before he found the chestnut again.

Cramming his pockets full of the extra ammunition, he draped the field glasses around his neck and started up the canyon. There would be no moon, but if it took longer than he hoped, they might come in handy after sunup.

If he lived that long.

22

Freed of the horse, Slocum was more mobile. He sprinted up the canyon in short bursts, stopping every hundred yards or so to make sure he hadn't lost the trail. The marks of so many hooves were not that easy to follow in the dry ground, but the little depressions in dust pockets were all he needed. At every possible digression, he moved more carefully, crouching to see which way the horses went. So far he'd been lucky. There was no sign that the Apaches had split up. If that happened, he'd be up a tree, because there was no way to tell which way Ginny would have been taken.

He was more than half a mile in now, and the early night was even darker down in the canyon than it had been the night before out in the flats. Muffling his footsteps as best he could, he tried to move as quickly as the need for silence permitted.

The ground was sloping upward gently, not enough to wind him but enough that he was aware of it. At three-quarters of a mile, he was almost directly below the spot where he'd waited for nightfall. The promontory was high above him. In a hundred yards, he would be directly below it, where the knife-edge of the point jutted away from an almost vertical wall.

In the darkness, it was like looking at a cliff made entirely of coal. Closer in, he could see more sharply, but every shadow was a potential hiding place, every rock a possible assailant. He became aware of his breathing—sharp, raspy, it dried his throat, and sounded like thunder as he trotted along.

Stopping once more, he had to get on hands and knees to see the ground clearly. Straight ahead, the canyon continued its gentle ascent. To his left, a passage between two towering boulders vanished in darkness black as pitch. To the right, another passage, barely wide enough to permit a man on horseback to slip through without bringing his legs up and over his mount's neck.

Which way to go? He looked up, as if for inspiration. A star just past the rimrock caught his eye. It was there, and then it was gone.

And then it was back.

Someone was moving along the rim! He couldn't see clearly enough, but it had to be a man. As he danced along the rim, he kept blocking out the glitter of one star after another, his own bulk dark as the sky behind it, leaving him all but undetectable.

So, they were still here. And that meant Ginny was still here, still close by. A sharp crack startled him, until he realized it was a fallen rock striking something below. Slocum crouched down even further, trying to blend in with the earth, stretching his body full length then, hoping not to be seen.

Lying on his back in the shadow of one of the boulders, he watched the man's progress. He couldn't even see enough detail to know whether it was an Apache. But who else could it be? In asking the question, he had already answered it.

For one giddy moment, he toyed with the notion of taking a shot at the man. But he was almost certain to miss, and the chance to surprise the Indians would be gone in one impulsive second.

He could see the shape of the man now, not clearly, but

well enough. The man had moved back to the promontory. Standing on the point, like a carved figurehead on the prow of a ship, the man was motionless for what seemed an eternity. Why? Slocum wondered. Had he made more noise than he thought? Had the Indians been watching him? Or were they just nervous?

And what good would knowing the answer be to him?

He heard something then. An owl maybe. Almost an owl, somewhere high above him. Then another, behind him, on the canyon floor. He held his breath, waiting for a repeat, but there was none.

A moment later, a stone cracked against another. And he heard the muffled sound of someone cursing himself. A hundred yards away, maybe less, he guessed. Slithering in among the stones, he got to his feet. He had a boot knife, and felt for it, bending no more than necessary to slide his hand inside the tight leather. It came away with a whisper, and he held it close to his thigh.

The man on the canyon floor was coming closer. He was almost certain to pass close by, maybe even within an arm's length. He heard the rasp of breathing, the whisper of soft leather on stone, and then it was behind him. Above him somehow, and then it was gone.

He turned in bewilderment, sorting through the explanations, dismissing each as it occurred to him. There was none that made sense. He took a deep breath and held it, thinking perhaps the Apache was waiting for him to show himself, to make a sound. Then he heard another rock break free, this time from higher up. Maybe on its own, maybe not, he thought. He looked up, but there was nothing but shadow above him, until he was looking straight up at the stars.

He crept back the way he'd come, a few yards at first, then ten. Finally, after fifteen yards, he found it. A slit in the rock, so narrow he'd missed it his first time past. He had to turn sideways to slide in. For a moment, the massive rock seemed to press against him as if it were moving ever so slightly. Then he was through.

Dropping to one knee again, he felt the ground with his fingertips, looking for an impression, some slight disturbance of the coating of fine silt. But there were too many fragments of rock. And something else caught his attention, a dimple in the dust, then another. Several in a string, like pearls. The dust clung to his fingers in a fine paste. Mud. Dripping water. The Apache had been filling canteens.

Slocum moved up a few yards, pausing every step to listen. The knife handle was getting slick with sweat, and he shifted hands to wipe his clammy palm on his shirt. Another ten yards, then ten more. There was total silence. Another ten yards and he kicked a pebble. It skittered away, clacked on the rocks below. Its echo sounded as if it would never die away. Then it was silent again, and Slocum allowed himself to breathe.

The incline was steep. Slocum had to lean forward to keep his balance. He was moving among huge slabs of stone, sometimes having to change direction, sometimes coming flush up against a wall. Groping with arms extended, he felt for the edge of the rock, then slid past and climbed another ten or fifteen yards. He was thankful he didn't have to run here. In the blackness he would have gotten no more than twenty or twenty-five yards before becoming hopelessly lost.

He climbed for nearly an hour, twice getting trapped in a blind alley and being forced to retrace his steps. Each twist and turn seemed exactly like all the others, and it was all he could do to remember which way he'd turned last. He kept watching the jumbled stone ahead, hoping for a break, anything to keep him from turning a corner and tripping over the Apaches.

He could look down into the canyon now, but it was impossible to see anything because the light was too feeble. So he pushed on like a blind man in a coal mine, finding his way by his fingertips. Another turn and he entered an open stretch. On tiptoe, he covered it as quickly as he could, then pressed himself against a slab of rock for a moment's rest.

Catching his breath he heard something, a cough maybe. He couldn't be sure. It sounded distant, but with the winding path he'd had to take, he couldn't be certain. Feeling along the slab, he reached the corner and listened intently. The sound wasn't repeated, but he was convinced he was getting close now.

Easy does it, he thought. Take your time. You've come too far to make a mistake now.

Glancing up, he saw a stone wall slanting up at a sharp angle, maybe fifty or fifty-five degrees. In the darkness, it was hard to tell just how far up the wall went. He moved toward it, the germ of an idea beginning to crystallize. Slocum leaned forward to feel the surface. From a distance, it looked almost smooth, but up close, he could see its texture was much rougher.

What the hell, he might as well try. He wished he had a sling for the Winchester, but it was too late to worry about that now. He shoved it through his belt in the back, letting it hang down like a tail every bit as deadly as that of a scorpion. Planting one foot on the wall, he leaned far forward and levered his other foot a few inches above the first, feeling for a foothold with the toe of his boot. He found one, then a second. Foot by foot, his body bent almost double, he managed to get nearly twenty feet up. It looked to be another twenty or thirty feet to the lip of the wall above him.

The climb was a gamble. He had no idea how much room, if any, he'd find at the top. Or what he would do once he got there. But his patience was running out. If he could get above the Apaches, he'd give himself an edge. It was a risk worth taking.

Using his hands for balance, he could feel the sharp edges of the folds of rock. In his mind's eye, he could see the layered colors, stacked like sheets of thick paper and torn off by an indifferent hand. Ten feet from the top the angle grew steeper. He was almost flat against the wall now, but he knew he could make it.

When his fingers curled over the ledge, he allowed him-

self a sigh of relief, then quickly hauled himself up and over.
He was on a stone shelf no more than ten or twelve feet wide
and some hundred feet long. Another wall, steeper than the
one he'd just climbed, loomed above him. For a moment,
he considered trying to scale it as well, but that was pushing
his luck. He moved to the shelf end back toward the flats. He
could get up higher that way, but only by jumping across a
break in the shelf and scaling a mound of boulders.

The other end was more promising. There was a break
in the shelf where a section of the stone had given way,
but it wasn't wide. Past the break, the shelf sloped up at
a scalable angle as far as he could see into the darkness.
Backing up, he took a tentative run and sprang as far out as
he could. He landed hard on his knees, but he'd made it.

Listening again, he heard nothing for a long minute, then
that same cough. And a voice now, a mumble really, but
someone talking. He tried to catch the words, but they were
too indistinct. Then silence again as whoever had spoken
lapsed back into quiet.

Slocum stayed on his knees, crawling along a few feet
at a time, sweeping the ground ahead with an open palm to
find a place for his knees among the sharp stones. Someone
coughed again, and this time the sound was almost directly
below him. He crept to the edge of the shelf and took off
his hat. Leaning out over the edge an inch or so, he peered
down into the darkness. Fifty feet below, barely discernible
in the pooled shadows, he saw a number of oblong shapes
which could have been stones.

And they could have been sleeping men.

He was determined to find out which.

Crawling back away from the edge, he pulled the Winchester from his belt and lay it against the base of the wall.
He leaned back against the stone to wait for sunrise. He was
bone tired, but he couldn't allow himself to fall asleep.

It was only an hour before dawn, and he wanted to hear
the first stirring from below. The sky grew slowly brighter
and the stars seemed to be extinguished by the handful until

only one or two could be seen. Below him though, it was still dark. The sun would have to come up before he'd be able to see clearly. He reached out almost absently to let his hand rest on the stock of the Winchester, as if unconsciously he needed to reassure himself that it was still there.

At a quarter to five, it was bright enough to see. Cautiously, he stretched. Every limb was stiff and sore. His back ached where the stone had dug into it for the last hour. Moving back to the edge, he looked out and down.

The Apaches were asleep. He counted them, stopping at four. Where was the fifth? And where was Ginny? He leaned out a little further, then further still, until he could look straight down along the wall.

There, huddled in a blanket, was the fifth Apache. And Ginny, her eyes wide, was staring back at him. He brought a finger to his lips.

She nodded slightly and closed her eyes again.

23

He wanted to open fire. They were so close, and such easy targets. But at the first shot, even assuming he got his target, the other four would be moving, and Ginny was bound and gagged, easy prey. There had to be some other way.

Where were their horses? he wondered. That had to be the key. If he could get to their mounts, he could keep them here. If they started to move again, it would be one more day of tracking them, one more day of risking discovery, one more day of terror for Ginny Settle. They could decide to kill her at any moment. But if they were forced to go on foot, the situation would change. The balance would tip Slocum's way, only a little maybe, but he needed every edge he could get.

Backing away from the edge of the shelf, he listened intently. The horses would be awake. They had to make noise. If they were within earshot, he had a chance to find them. Slocum looked up at the next wall. In daylight, he might just make it, but he didn't know where it would lead. Instead, he moved along the shelf and started up the steep incline.

Fifty feet higher, he could look down into the camp and see half of the Apaches. So far, none had stirred. The incline grew steeper, then ended in a sheer face nearly a dozen feet high. To his right, a seam in the rock ran down to within half a dozen feet of the shelf. If he could just get up high enough, he could use it to negotiate the last six feet.

It was wide enough for his fingers, and he tried to get a handhold, but a chunk of rock broke away in his hands. He caught it in the air, let his breath out slowly, to steady his nerves, then set the rock on the ground. Trying again, he got a grip deeper inside the seam. Slocum pulled himself up by sheer force, his body bent into a U as he braced the soles of his boots against the rock and levered himself up high enough to grab another handhold.

It was slow going, and it felt as if his arms were about to tear loose, but in fifteen minutes he was close enough to get one hand on the top of the wall. Changing his grip, he slapped at the ledge with his other hand, while his body swung forward and slammed into the wall. The impact nearly dislodged him, but his belt buckle caught on an outcropping, and took enough weight for him to adjust his grip.

Using what he was convinced was the last bit of energy in his aching body, he pulled himself up and over the edge. The going was easier now, and he climbed to the promontory. From there, he would be able to see the canyon and, if luck was with him, the Apache horses. It took another ten minutes. As he reached the promontory, he took off his hat and crept out to the point.

Using the glasses again, he could see the still-sleeping Apaches. Only now, there were four. Where was the fifth? He scanned the canyon quickly, but could see no sign of the missing Indian. Far below, he could see the pond near where the bay and the chestnut were tethered by the creek.

But there was no sign of the Apache horses. And now he'd lost track of one of the bucks. He turned to crawl back from the edge when he heard a grunt. Somebody was coming. Probably the buck, coming to take a look at the canyon.

There was no place to hide. Slocum pulled his boot knife and moved back toward the trail. He started down, looking for cover. A cluster of large rocks to the left was his only hope. He sprinted for the rocks and dove over the nearest, landing hard on his right shoulder and losing his grip on the knife. It clattered among the rocks, then slipped down into a crevice.

Rubbing his shoulder, he crawled toward the crevice. He could get his hand down into it and just barely brushed the handle, but there wasn't enough room to curl his fingers around it. The knife moved as he withdrew his hand, sliding another inch or so into the crack. Using two fingers like a pair of pliers, he managed to squeeze the handle, but when he tried to pull the knife out, it slipped from his grasp. He could hear the Apache now, breathing heavily and making no attempt to conceal his approach.

He had to have the knife, dammit! Pincering the handle again, he squeezed the handle even tighter. This time, instead of trying to pull it straight out, he wiggled it back and forth, trying to loosen it. When the handle was so far over to the left, almost horizontal, he was able to pull the blade free. Maneuvering the knife to the left a little more he had enough room for his fingers to curl under the handle.

He pulled and the knife came out, nearly slipping away again, but he caught it before it could fall back. Getting into a crouch, he got ready to spring on the Apache, but the noise had stopped. A moment later, it started again, this time behind him. He turned to see the Apache balancing on some rocks above him, but so far unaware that Slocum was right below.

Then the Indian was gone. Slocum scrambled out of the rocks and moved down the trail until he found a narrow cut. He entered it, then climbed up and over a slab of red stone. He could just see the top of the Apache's head now, moving away from him. Slocum moved quickly. He had the knife in one hand, the Winchester, a last resort, in the other.

He felt like a burglar in broad daylight, as if any moment a heavy hand would descend onto his shoulder and jerk him back. He was twenty-five yards behind the Apache, who still seemed oblivious to his presence. The ground sloped sharply upward, and the Apache dropped out of sight. As Slocum reached the top, he found himself staring into a shallow depression full of thick grass. It wasn't more than a hundred yards across. And there, munching contentedly, were the Apache horses.

Slocum watched the warrior closely. He wasn't sure why the Indian had come up alone. And he wondered how the horses had gotten up in the first place. They couldn't have come the way Slocum and the Apache had gotten there, which meant there had to be another way down, one the horses could negotiate. The brave unhobbled one of the mounts, took the rawhide strand and looped it over the horse's tail. Tugging to be sure it was secure, he moved to the next animal and knotted the free end of the thong through its halter.

One by one, he tied the animals together. Slocum used the time to move along the edge of the shallow valley. Halfway around, he found what he was looking for. A gap in the rocks led down along a narrow path. He could see hoofprints in the dust. Slocum started down, certain now the Apache would be coming this way.

The trail was narrow, with a steep wall on one side and a rock-littered slope on the other. The only place he could conceal himself was on top of the wall. Slocum jumped to catch the lip, hauled himself up and then crept back as far as he could, pressing himself down onto the narrow rock shelf. Raising his head just enough to get a look at the Apache, he saw that all the animals had been lashed together now. While he watched, he saw the Apache move back to the lead horse and climb into the saddle.

The warrior squeezed his horse between his knees, kicking it with his moccasined heels, and started to turn. Slocum pressed himself down, trying desperately to keep below the Indian's line of sight. He knew what he had to do now, and that his timing had to be perfect. And it would have to be done blind. If he raised his head too soon, the Apache would spot him.

Slocum listened to the approaching hooves, trying to gauge the distance. He heard the first hooves leave the grass and strike on stone. That meant the buck was thirty-five feet away. The sound of the clopping hooves came closer, growing even louder as another of the horses left the grass and stepped onto the rocky ground.

He rubbed his thumb nervously on the knife handle, then shifted his legs closer to the rock on his right. Coiling his legs like springs, he changed his grip on the knife once more. Closer now, just ten feet to go, then five. And he pushed.

Sliding toward the edge of the rock shelf, the rasp of his clothing and scrape of his belt buckle alerted the Apache, who was looking straight up at him as Slocum went over the edge. He had gauged it well, catching the Apache with his left arm as he went by, and pulling the man from his horse.

The Apache went for a pistol in his belt and Slocum kicked up hard, going for the groin and missing, but knocking the pistol loose. The Apache sprang at him then and Slocum rolled. He went on over the edge and spread his arms as he slid partway down the scree-covered slope, the Apache right behind him. He had lost his grip on the Winchester, and saw it several feet up the slope.

The buck tried to stand, but the loose debris gave him no footing, and his feet went out from under him. Slocum held the knife out at arm's length, and the Apache narrowly avoided impaling himself on the upturned blade.

But Slocum had the edge he needed. He rolled to his right, scissoring his legs around the scrambling warrior and preventing him from getting up. He slashed out with the knife, caught the Apache on the upper arm and ripped viciously to the right. He felt the blade strike bone and the Apache opened his mouth, ready to shout for help. Slocum kicked him in the mouth, and he felt the crunch of breaking teeth, turning the shouts to a croak.

The Indian landed on his back in the scree, and slid several feet, his arms flailing as he tried to stop the skid. Slocum was on him immediately. The Apache drew his own blade, an ugly-looking bowie knife, and Slocum clamped his left hand around the Apache's right wrist, and brought his own knife down once, then twice.

The Apache groaned, then lay still. Slocum jerked his knife free, and wiped the bloody blade in the dirt. He grabbed the bowie knife and stuck it in his belt. The riderless horses had stopped twenty yards down the trail. They were skittish, and Slocum approached them slowly. The least sudden movement might send them on down the trail. They were a liability now, and he had to do something about it quickly. If he cut them loose, they might alert the others. If he brought them back and hobbled them, chances were the Apaches would send someone else for them when the first man failed to return. But he couldn't sit there all day and wait. He had no choice.

He moved gingerly to the front of the line. Shaking his head, he withdrew the bowie knife and brought it up sharply into the chest of the lead horse. He wiggled the blade, looking for the heart, found it, and jerked the knife free as the animal snorted once then fell to its knees.

Down the line he went, one by one, until all six horses lay dead. He felt sick to his stomach, repelled by the slaughter, and walked slowly back down along the carcasses. He couldn't bring himself to look at the dead animals.

He had improved the odds, but he felt no elation. Stepping past the last horse, he bent and almost absently patted its motionless flanks, then headed down the path without looking back. Working his way down the trail, he retrieved his Winchester, keeping an ear open for any sound from below. If any of the others were awake, and they almost certainly were, one might shout to his tribesman. When no answer was received, all hell would break loose. He had to be in position before that happened.

Almost before he realized it, he found himself staring straight into the camp. It was directly below him now, down a steep incline. Ginny was still bound, her body curved in toward the wall. A single Apache sat a few feet away, loading his pistol.

There was no way to get to him without noise. Slocum crouched behind a rock, knowing he was going to have to use his gun, and knowing that the sooner he did, the better off he would be. He brought the Winchester up and drew a bead on the center of the Apache's chest.

As he cocked the hammer back, the click must have registered, because the Indian's hands froze in midair, his head turned to the right. It was just starting back to the left when Slocum fired. The Apache slammed back against the wall, and Ginny turned her head to see what had happened.

Slocum was already halfway across the clearing by the time she saw him. He cut the ropes around her ankles and hauled her to her feet. He ran to the dead Indian and grabbed his pistol. A carbine lay on the ground beside him, and Slocum took it, too. He remembered the Apaches dividing a load of ammunition, but there was no time to look for the bullets.

He grabbed Ginny by the arm and tugged her back the way he'd come. It was away from their mounts, but it was the only place he was sure there were no Apaches. Ginny stumbled, and Slocum had to half-carry her for several feet. Only when they had gone fifty or sixty yards did he stop, and then just long enough to cut the rope binding her hands in front of her.

She jerked the gag from her mouth, then rubbed her wrists to try to restore circulation.

"Where are the others?" Slocum whispered, tugging on her arm.

Ginny was limping from having been bound so tightly, and she was terrified. "I don't know," she said, her eyes welling up. "One went for the horses. I don't know where the others are."

"We've got to find them," Slocum said. "Before they find us."

24

Slocum checked the Apache's Winchester. It was fully loaded. Handing it to Ginny, he asked, "You know how to use this?"

She looked at him with glazed eyes for a moment. Then as if suddenly aware of an insulting question, she snatched the rifle away. "You bet I do," she said.

He pointed to some broken rock back toward the point. "Let's go," he said, taking her by the hand. When they reached the rocks, he pushed her down behind the largest of them. "Stay here. Whatever happens, don't come out. Use the rifle only if you have to. I don't want you giving your position away."

"And what are you going to do?"

"I have horses for the two of us, but there are three Apache bucks between us and them. There's only one thing *to* do."

He started to back out and she reached out a hand. "Slocum," she whispered, "be careful."

He nodded, then turned away. "I will be."

"If you don't come back, or if they get too close, I'm going to jump," she hissed. "I won't go through this anymore."

He turned again. The set of her jaw told him she meant it. "I'll be back," he said.

He sprinted toward the trail head, anxious to get into the rocks before the Apaches took it into their heads to come up looking for the horses. He wanted as much distance between him and Ginny as he could get. As long as she was out of harm's way, they had a chance. But if they caught her again, his hands would be tied. Ginny seemed to know that, and he almost smiled thinking of the determination in her face.

The sun was all the way up and by now the bucks had to know something was wrong. The gunshot was the tip-off. By now, they would have found their dead tribesman. As he moved past the scree-littered slope, he saw the body of the second warrior, and he had an idea. It would take time, but it just might make the difference. Slipping and sliding over the loose soil, he scrambled down to the corpse and sat beside it. He stripped the Apache's thigh-length moccasins and crawled back up the slope. Finding a pocket among the boulders, he sat down to pull off his boots and pull on the moccasins.

When he stood, it felt awkward to him. He was used to the high bootheels, and his first tentative steps felt to him like those of a drunk. He tucked the boots out of sight, and started down again.

The high ground would have been better, but he had to get to the Apaches before they found his horses. They had no food and very little water, and a prolonged siege was out of the question. He had to move quickly, and he couldn't afford to wait for nightfall. After dark, he'd lose whatever edge he had. And making a break for it on foot would just get them both killed. No, it was better to take the fight to the Apaches. As long as he was on the offensive, he had a chance.

He was getting used to the moccasins by the time he'd gone fifty yards. Not only were they much quieter than his boots, but they also disguised his passage. Seeing a moccasin print would not alert the Apaches the way a boot print would. Now, all he had to do was find them.

Slocum knew he couldn't go much further down into the canyon, because he'd be too far from Ginny, and run the added risk of letting the Indians get above him. But he couldn't sit and wait, either. He still had the glasses, and he bent to scoop a handful of the dusty soil. Crouching behind a rock, he tilted the lenses slightly upward and licked them, then sprinkled the dust on the glass.

Tilting them again to let the excess run off, he tried to look through them, but too much had clung to the moisture. He tilted them again to blow off a little. Trying again, he was satisfied. He could see well enough, and the fine coating would cut down the chance of a reflection giving him away. He turned then and looked back up toward the rocky point, picking up the path he'd taken earlier about a hundred yards from the top.

He checked it all the way up, saw nothing, and started working the glasses back down. Nothing. Where the hell were they? He let the glasses fall and started to get to his feet when he heard something below him, off the trail. Hunkering down behind the rocks again, he listened carefully. But he didn't hear it again.

Just behind him, a gigantic slab of stone, fifteen feet across and twice as long, leaned back against a steep wall of rock. Slocum moved to its edge, then ducked down along beside it. It was nearly a dozen feet thick, and there was just enough room for him to squeeze along the edge back toward the wall.

He could climb now, using one edge of the slab and the rocks to his right to get up near the top. Standing on the flat edge of a ragged column, he could just reach the top edge of the slab. The moccasins gave him a better grip on the rock, and he managed to clamber up and over. He found himself in a V-shaped depression filled with fine sand. It gave him good visibility and some cover, but his maneuverability was severely restricted.

Then he saw the Apache. The warrior was working his way among the rocks, taking a path parallel to the trail but some fifteen feet to its right, climbing from rock to rock. The Apache was still a hundred feet or more downhill from him, as Slocum brought his Winchester around. The Indian dropped off a tall rock, flashed briefly between it and a second, smaller rock, then disappeared.

Counting the seconds, Slocum tracked with the gunsight, waiting for a target. He saw the warrior again, but the man stopped and backtracked for some reason. Slocum moved his sight back to the narrow gap, knowing as he did so that a shot at the opening was pointless. By the time the Apache's presence registered and he squeezed the trigger, the Indian would already be past.

Reluctantly, he lowered the rifle. That's when he heard the noise behind him. He rolled on his back and looked up. Perched on a rock high above him, his body outlined with fire by the sun right behind him, Slocum saw a second buck. The Indian hadn't seen him yet, but it wouldn't be long.

Bringing the Winchester to bear, he sighted on the bright red headband holding the Apache's straight black hair in place. The moment was frozen as Slocum watched, wondering whether the buck would move and which way. He took a deep breath as the warrior started to crouch, and Slocum was glad he'd held his fire. He blinked away tears as the brilliant sunlight momentarily blinded him. As Slocum squinted away the pain, the Apache, leaning forward to balance himself with his fingertips, coiled himself, getting ready to jump.

The thick legs tensed and Slocum squeezed. The rifle butt slammed into his shoulder and the Apache straightened awkwardly, his jump aborted, then misdirected. The bullet had done some damage, but not much, or the warrior would have fallen. Slocum jerked the lever and fired again as the Indian turned his head, looking for the source of the previous shot. This time, the bullet slammed home, striking bone and tipping the Indian off balance. His hands clawed the air for a moment, and then he was gone.

Slocum heard the body thud into the rocks below, drowning out the fading echo of the gunshot. Then it got perfectly quiet. Slocum blinked away the bright glare, his eyes burning from the white-hot sun.

As soon as his vision cleared, he turned his attention to the trail. He had to move. He slid down the front of the slab, sprinted twenty yards downhill, zigzagging among the rocks. There was still no sign of the Apache he'd seen below. And there was a third man out there somewhere, one he hadn't yet seen. But one who might have seen him and who might already be circling in for the kill.

He debated standing pat, but it was too risky. If he'd been seen, he'd play right into their hands. As long as he kept moving, he could keep them off balance. He reached the turn now, where he could head down onto the rock shelf above the Apache camp. Without thinking, he changed direction. He slid down the rocks on his rump, trying to stay low and still move as quickly as possible. Sprinting now, he leaped the gap, landed lightly on his toes, and raced the length of the shelf.

There had to be a way to smoke them out, he thought. And he glanced up at the point. He wondered for a second how Ginny was faring, but brushed the worry away. He had to keep his mind clear and focused. How could he get them to show themselves?

Hefting a hunk of stone in his left hand, he tossed it down among the rocks, heard it clatter a few feet, then stop. A moment later, he caught a flash of black a few feet away from where the rock had landed. Was it hair?

Slocum ducked down, then groped for another rock without taking his eyes off the spot. He grabbed a stone the size of his fist. He tossed it in a high arc, knowing that if it were seen in the air, it might give his location away.

The stone landed with a sharp crack, and again he saw the glimpse of black. This time he knew it was hair. His first impulse was to climb down over the rocks, but he couldn't do it without exposing himself, and he would need both hands for several seconds. He would be unable to hold a weapon.

He crept along the shelf a few feet, trying to get a better angle, but there was no sign of the Apache now. Another rock would accomplish nothing. All he could do was wait for the man to show himself. And hope the missing Apache wasn't somewhere above him.

Patience was not Slocum's long suit. As the seconds ticked off, turned into minutes, and seemed to drag on into eternity, he kept sweeping his gaze along a stretch of rocks below. Somewhere in that jumbled mass was another Apache. The man couldn't get out without exposing himself, but Slocum couldn't move, either, and time was on the Apache's side.

He could try to find the second Indian, but he was reluctant to give up the bird in hand. Moving back to the break in the shelf, he lay on his belly and peered out over the edge. Looking straight down, he saw enough outcroppings to take the chance. It was a straight drop, nearly thirty feet, but directly below him the ground was fairly level. If he could just get halfway down, he could drop the remaining fifteen feet.

Pivoting without raising himself up, he let his legs dangle over the edge. Bending his body, he brought his feet up against the face of the drop. The toes scraped and scratched, looking for something to bite on. With the Winchester tucked in the back of his belt, he took the plunge. Hanging by his fingertips, he managed to find a chunk of stone big enough to get a foothold on and secure enough to take his weight.

A few inches below the edge, another chunk of stone jutted out of the rock face. He reached for it, and put some weight on it, but it pulled loose and cracked on the stone below him. He cursed under his breath, then reached for the cavity the fallen stone had left behind. The outer edge crumbled away, but there was enough for him to grab onto.

He lowered himself down, staying flat against the wall, giving the handhold his trust. Foot by foot, he climbed down the sheer rock face. Twelve feet above the ground, he ran out of handholds. He'd already taken his eyes off the Apache's hiding place for too long. Pushing out and away from the wall, he let go and steeled himself for the impact.

He landed hard, and the soft leather of the moccasins did little to protect his feet. But nothing broke. Darting through the abandoned camp, he kept to the wall, stepping over the dead Apache without looking. It was nearly two hundred yards to a point where he could pick up the trail from below now, and he sprinted in a crouch, looking up every couple of steps, until he reached the turn.

The Apache was above him now, maybe three hundred yards. That was a lot of ground to sacrifice. He hoped it proved to be worth it. Entering the trail, he moved the first hundred yards at full tilt. But as he closed the gap, he slowed, then left the trail altogether, moving from rock to rock, going up and over boulders where he had to, or where skirting them would require him to reenter the narrow trail.

He was close now, within pistol range. But so far he had seen no further sign of the Apache. If the buck had abandoned his hiding place, Slocum had lost him altogether. The consequences of such a mistake were incalculable. He crossed his fingers and whispered a short prayer.

If his memory hadn't misled him, the Apache was on the other side of a slab of stone lying on its edge just ahead. On tiptoe, he bulled ahead, his Colt Navy drawn and cocked. He was closing fast when he tripped and fell. The gun clattered away and he scrambled after it on all fours.

As his fingers closed over the butt, he saw movement out of the corner of his eye, a shadow on the pale ground. Instinctively, he rolled left. A split second later, a gun went off, and as he rolled he saw the Apache thirty feet above him, clinging to a rock wall with one hand, his body turned awkwardly at right angles to the face.

Slocum rolled again and came up firing. His first shot missed, spanging off the rock inches to the Indian's left. As he fired a second time, the Apache let go, kicked the wall with his feet and arced out and down, barreling for Slocum headfirst. He cartwheeled once in midair, now coming down feetfirst. Slocum backed away, but the Apache brushed him on the way past, knocking him to the ground.

The Indian had landed on his feet and sprang at Slocum as he tried to get up. Slocum took the full weight as the buck launched himself, but kicked up and over, catapulting the Apache into the boulders behind him.

The Indian was stunned by the blow and Slocum cocked the Colt Navy as he tried to get up. The gun went off and the Apache's eyes opened wide, as if he hadn't expected it. He slid down off the boulder, his weight bending his head at an odd angle, and lay still.

Now there was one to go.

25

Where was the last Apache? Slocum kept asking himself the question over and over again as he raced back through the winding maze toward the top of the mountain. He wanted to get back to Ginny now. With one warrior remaining, they could take a chance on getting to the horses. The buck would be no match for them on foot.

He took the same narrow trail back up, a reckless, headlong dash that left him gasping for air with every step. He knew he was being less careful than he should be, not even bothering to check every little pocket and slowing only to negotiate the more demanding turns in the circuitous path. But if he got to Ginny first, there was no chance she could be taken hostage and used against him.

He was only a hundred yards from the top when he spotted the buck out of the corner of his eye. The Indian was climbing a sheer stone wall to the promontory. Spread-eagled against the steep face like a four-legged spider, he was less than twenty feet from the top, the shiny new carbine hanging down his back from a makeshift sling.

Slocum skidded to a halt and dropped to one knee. As if he sensed something, the Apache started moving more quickly. His legs bent awkwardly as he moved from foothold to foothold, his hands slapping at the rock and pulling his upper body closer and closer to the rimrock.

Slocum took careful aim. The lead sight was centered on the Apache's spine, right between the shoulder blades. He took a deep breath, held it. And squeezed. The report of the carbine sounded strangely muted, a cough instead of a bang. The bullet fell far short of the target, hitting the wall nearly ten yards below the Indian's feet.

It was a bad load. Slocum cursed and jerked the ejection lever but no shell came out. Twice more, he jerked the lever and twice more no spent cartridge was ejected. He could see the end of it, but there wasn't enough showing for him to get hold of it. The casing must have split, he thought, and the ejector couldn't pull it free. Three more times he worked the lever, still to no effect.

He reached for his Colt Navy, but it was a long shot for a handgun. The Apache was almost to the rim now. Another three feet and he'd be able to grab the edge and haul himself up and over. Slocum fired the Colt, but the shot went wide, chipping stone to the Apache's left. The brave never even turned to look back. He had his hands full as it was, and if he lost his grip, it was seventy or eighty feet to the rocks below him.

Slocum admired the Apache's concentration, even as he aimed and fired a second time. But he'd overcompensated, and the bullet narrowly missed the Apache's right arm. A second later, and the climbing warrior got his left hand up onto the rim. His right followed as Slocum aimed once more.

The Apache's feet were braced on a small shelflike outcropping, and he bent his legs slightly as Slocum fired, then propelled himself up until his body bent forward, leaving his legs dangling out over the abyss. Slocum's shot went high and hit nothing at all. A second later, the Apache disappeared over the rim.

Slocum broke into a run, concentrating now on the rimrock and the promontory. The Indian knew he was down there and Slocum expected to see him reappear at any moment. But with every step he took, Slocum was less certain. When he'd gone twenty yards, there had still been no sign of the Apache.

And the same damn question came back to haunt him once more. Where was the last Apache?

Slocum's legs felt like they had been dipped in molten iron. His joints ached from the pounding, and his muscles were on the verge of cramping. He was puffing like a steam engine, each inhalation spreading liquid fire across his chest. The closer to the top he came, the steeper the ascent. The last fifty yards were the worst. His legs were losing their coordination. He had to slow down or risk a fall.

His mouth felt like he'd been eating sandpaper, his tongue was a slab of old leather against his dry and brittle lips. He still had the Winchester and thought about discarding it to get rid of the dead weight. But he knew he might need it, if he managed to get through this latest trial.

He saw the Apache then, suddenly erect, his carbine rising to his shoulder. Slocum dodged to the right as the Indian fired. The bullet ricocheted off a rock in front of him and Slocum dove in among the boulders. His knee cracked against the stone, and a stab of pain lanced up through his thigh. As he tried to get into a crouch, he realized the leg had gone numb. As he pulled himself deeper into the rocks, the limb dragged behind him, useless.

Slocum sat with his back against the rocks, rubbing the knee, trying to squeeze life back into it. He could bend it, and his fingers told him the kneecap was intact. Must have hit a nerve, he thought. It would come back all right, but maybe not soon enough.

Two more shots cracked high above him. Both bullets slammed into the boulders, but neither was close. The Apache couldn't see him and was trying to smoke him out. A ricochet could kill him just as dead as a direct hit, and he lay on his stomach, clawing at the ground with both hands. Another bullet found its way in among the stones, this time burying itself in the rocky soil.

Using the rocks to pull himself along, Slocum twisted and turned like a snake to negotiate the tight turns among the boulders. He was almost twenty feet from his first location, but still not out of the woods. He tried to raise his head, but another shot nicked the brim of his hat and he ducked down again. And now the Apache knew where he was.

The feeling in his leg was returning, but it was a slow process. He could flex it without as much pain, and the joint seemed undamaged, but there was still no way the leg would bear his weight, not in a flat-out sprint. He might be able to hobble a few feet, but that would do him little good.

To get a clear shot, he'd have to expose himself again to the warrior's carbine. Before he could risk that, he had to be able to move. Massaging the knee again, he felt waves of pain as he kept hitting a tender spot to the left of the kneecap. Slocum tried pushing himself along the ground, flexing the knee and bracing his foot against a rock, but the knee buckled as soon as he applied pressure.

Cursing under his breath, he tried again. Again the knee gave way. It took a little more pressure this time, but still nowhere near enough to support his weight. And running on it was out of the question. He knew the leg would come back, but he didn't have time to wait. And if the Apache sensed that he was hurt, he would move in for the kill.

For one giddy moment, he thought about crawling out into the open, to decoy the buck and draw him closer. But it was a stupid risk. There was no reason the Apache wouldn't stay right where he was. And unable to move, Slocum would be helpless as a fish in a barrel.

Slocum pulled the Winchester alongside and pulled the ejection lever all the way back. There was no time to disassemble the weapon. He took his boot knife and scratched at the rim of the jammed cartridge. It resisted at first, but slowly he saw a gap between the rim and breech wall. With enough space, he was able to get the blade point in and dig it into the cartridge wall. The empty shell finally popped free.

He checked it, saw where the rim had been sliced down to the cartridge wall, just enough for it to slip off the ejector. He wondered whether it was an accident or whether someone had tampered with the .44-caliber shells before they were sold to the Apaches. It wouldn't take much to cause the gun to jam, and you didn't have to tamper with many. Just a couple here and there. Sooner or later, the rifle would jam. Slocum worked the lever until his magazine was empty. One more of the cartridges had been tampered with. He tossed it away, then reloaded, filling the magazine with additional ammunition from his own supply.

Trying the knee again, he found it flexed normally, and the numbness was just about gone. He was able to put weight on it now, but it would still be difficult to run, and if he had to pivot on the knee, chances were better than even it would buckle under him.

In frustration, he slapped at the kneecap, trying by force of will to restore it to full function, but it was useless. He'd just have to be patient. Wriggling around a boulder, he looked up at the promontory, half-expecting a slug to come smashing into the rock beside his head. But nothing happened. Cautiously, he crept an inch or two forward, enough to let him get a look at the rocky point.

It was deserted. A moment later, he heard a piercing shriek. He thought at first the Apache had stumbled on Ginny's hiding place, but as the cry registered more clearly, he realized the voice was too deep. It was that of a man. Half rage and half anguish, the cry seemed to waft out over the canyon and flow down into it. It seemed as if it would never end, as if the screaming man would not stop until the canyon was full to its very rim with the horrendous sound of his pain and anger.

The horses, Slocum thought. He's found the horses.

Hauling himself up, he tried to walk normally, but his leg wouldn't cooperate. Using the Winchester as a cane, he hobbled out from behind the rocks and started uphill. Every step sent a drop of molten lead coursing through the knee, but he kept on moving, afraid that if he stopped he wouldn't be able to move again. As it was, if he fell, he knew he would never be able to get up in time.

The Winchester was so short, he had to stoop over to let it take his weight. He felt like a foolish old man running to catch his own hearse. But he didn't stop. He couldn't stop. If the Apache found Ginny now, there was no telling what he'd do.

As he neared the last and steepest leg of the trail, his knee started to throb, but he hopped on his good leg a couple of steps for every step on the bad left leg. Ten feet from the top, his sweaty hands lost their grip on the rifle and he fell on his face, rapping the bad knee on a rock the size and shape of a small skull. The gun fell beside him, starting to slide back the way he'd come. He reached for it, missed, and brought a foot down hard, catching the ejection lever with his toe.

Turning on his back, he managed to keep control of the rifle and sat up until he could reach the butt with his outstretched fingers. Bending his bad leg, he got the rifle close enough to grab, ignoring the searing pain in the knee. He heard something above and behind him and lay back to look up toward the point.

The Apache was standing there watching him. His face was a mask of intense hatred. The carbine in his hand dangled loosely as Slocum reached for his Colt. There was a sharp crack and the Indian looked stunned for a moment. Half-turning his body, he reached behind his back with one hand, then continuing his turn there was another crack, and this time Slocum saw the small geyser of blood, dark as oil in the bright sunlight, more like a shadow than a fluid.

The Apache staggered back one step, then another, his feet reaching now for support that wasn't there. His body seemed to collapse like a tube of soft cloth, and then he tumbled off the rock. He fell without a sound, slamming into an outcropping halfway down the sheer face of the cliff, changing direction, his limbs flapping like those of a doll, and then he was gone. When he hit bottom, a single sharp slap, like the clap of a hand, echoed dully off the canyon walls for just an instant.

A moment later, Ginny appeared on the promontory. She held Slocum's rifle crooked in her right elbow, looking for all the world like someone just finishing a successful hunt. Slocum started to crawl the rest of the way up the trail. Ginny saw him, put a hand to her mouth, once again the frightened young woman abducted by savage red men, and backed away from the point.

He heard her footsteps rushing over the broken ground, and then she was at the trail head, racing downhill toward him.

"Are you all right, Slocum? Please tell me you're all right. . . ."

He nodded. "Okay, I'm okay. I banged my knee, that's all." He pulled the bowie knife from his belt. "Here, see if you can find something to make a cane, would you?"

"I guess this means you won't be carrying me down like a real hero, then." She leaned over and kissed him on the top of his head. "You're still my favorite though, don't worry."

Then, as if the full impact of what had just happened sank in, her lips started to tremble. Tears welled up in her eyes, and she sniffed but made no attempt to wipe away the trickles as they streaked her dusty cheeks.

26

The descent was slow going. Using a makeshift crutch, Slocum had to stop every fifty or sixty yards. He kept grinding his teeth with the pain each time he was forced to use the bad leg instead of the crutch. As they descended, Slocum told Ginny about the tampered ammunition, about the rifles and about the skinny man with the ginger mustache who had provided the weapons.

"We have to tell someone," she said. "Somebody will know who he is. Somebody has to stop him. And I hope to God he hangs."

Slocum nodded. "He will. You can bet on it."

After three hours, they were almost at the canyon floor, and Slocum was looking forward to an extended rest before having to ride. They were both hot and sweaty, near exhaustion. Ginny offered to go for the horses, but Slocum shook his head. "No, I'd rather walk. It's not far now."

"You're crazy, you know that," she said. Stepping up to him she wrapped her arms around him, crutch and all. He winced and she stepped back, a crooked grin on her face. "You are crazy."

He smiled. "You'd never find them anyhow," he said. He was now feeling a little light-headed, and didn't know whether it was the pain and exhaustion of the descent or the flood of relief over the Apaches having been dealt with.

Either way, he didn't care. It was all over.

He hobbled the last leg across the canyon floor, then led Ginny in among the trees where the horses had been hidden. They were still there, munching contentedly.

He lowered himself to a thick carpet of grass along the creek bank, right where it flowed out of the pool carved by the falling water. Ginny stood back, hands on hips, looking up at the cascading water.

"It's breathtaking," she said. "Just beautiful. Who would have thought something like that could be out here in the middle of nowhere?"

She sat down and pulled off her boots, tossing them playfully in Slocum's direction. On hands and knees, she crawled toward him. "We have to take a look at that knee," she said, reaching for one of the moccasins. Taking the fringed top of the left moccasin, she started to roll it down his leg, taking care not to put any pressure on the knee. "You look kind of good in these things," she laughed.

When both moccasins were off, she shook her head. "Gonna have to do better than that, Slocum. Off with your pants." When he made no move to comply, she reached for the buckle of his gunbelt. He knew she was not going to be denied, so he unbuckled the gunbelt, then his dungarees. Flat on his back, he watched her tug the pants down, the tip of her tongue squeezed between her lips.

When the knee came into view, he winced at the sight of it. Ginny made a face. "That's ugly," she said. "Really ugly." The knee was swollen to almost twice its normal size. The kneecap was buried in the swollen flesh now, a depression shaped like a saucer instead of the usual raised disk. "You sure it's not broken?" she asked.

"No, just badly bruised."

"Maybe if you soak it," she said.

Slocum shook his head. "It won't help. I just have to stay off it."

"Maybe it won't help, but it won't hurt, either. You are rather ripe, Mr. Slocum. And so am I, for that matter."

"When we get someplace civilized, maybe," Slocum said.

"A civilized person doesn't take his cues from his surroundings, Mr. Slocum. Quite the reverse. I learned that in school."

"That was back East."

"It's still true." She tilted her head to one side. "You're nervous about me, aren't you?"

"Let's just say I'm nervous, period, and let it go at that."

Ginny grew solemn for a moment. "So much death, so much horror," she said. "It makes me feel so dirty. Like I . . . oh, I don't know . . . let's not talk about it." Then she laughed. "You remember a few weeks ago, when I asked you to wait with me while I took a swim?"

He nodded.

"Well, this time, you can't run away." She stood and started on her buttons. The shirt came away quickly, sticking to her skin in places where it had been soaked with sweat, then coming away with the sound of tearing paper. She slipped out of her jeans and stood before him, the pale skin streaked with dirt in many places.

Turning her back, she padded to the edge of the pool. He watched her bend to scoop handfuls of water from the pool and rub them over her skin. Without looking back at him, she said, "It's not at all cold. It feels rather good, actually."

Then she waded toward the waterfall and a moment later she was soaked from head to foot. The falling water nearly hid her behind a blue-white sheet. As she moved, an arm would deflect the sheet here and there, giving him glimpses of her body all the more tantalizing for their indistinctness.

A bent knee protruded through the screen of water, sending a fan of spray showering off in every direction. It caught the sunlight spilling down into the canyon, and a small rainbow arched across her middle. She was giggling like a schoolgirl.

Poking her head through the spray, her hair plastered to

her head and dangling down over her chest, she called to him. "Come on, Slocum. It feels wonderful."

When he didn't answer, she pulled her head back behind the cascade for a moment, then a single foot appeared, then a calf, a knee and, finally, one muscular thigh. She waggled the leg in a parody of a dancehall girl's seduction, her laughter echoing off the wall of rock behind her.

When that didn't work, she changed her tack. Using her arms as a screen she parted the waters until the full glory of her body was visible from shoulders to knees. She cocked one hip then, and gave a slight twist, just enough to get her full breasts bouncing. "Last chance," she called.

Slocum looked at her body, then at his knee, then back at her body. She was standing in front of the cascade now, hands on hips. Her skin shone in the sunlight. Beads of water sparkled like jewels on her coppery bush.

"You should come out now," he said. But his voice was tight, and she knew why.

"Come and get me." With that, she waded into shallower water and sat down. The water came up to her breasts, buoying them slightly, and they bobbed on the gentle current. Her prominent nipples were hard, their dark aureoles even darker against her whiteness.

Slocum raised himself to a sitting position and peeled off his shirt. His fingers fumbled with the buttons, and she laughed at him. He lay back down to tug off his underwear, then crawled toward the water.

As he slid in, the water felt good on his skin. He crept into deeper water, then walked on his hands until he was within a few feet of her. She stood then, and backed away a couple of steps. He looked up with a pained expression. Ginny shook her head and laughed. "You're not getting near me until you get cleaned off," she said.

As Ginny backed up, the water slowly climbed her legs, then rose suddenly to her hips. Following after her, Slocum found himself in water deep enough to swim in. He took a few strokes and then went under. When he came up, tossing his head to get the hair out of his eyes, Ginny was standing right by the cascade. "Over here, Mr. Slocum," she teased. "There's no soap, but we'll just have to make the best of it."

In front of the waterfall, he found he could stand. The water enabled him to hold himself on his good leg, just using the toes of his left foot to keep his balance. Ginny glided toward him, using her palm to send sheets of water arcing over his head and into his face.

He closed his eyes and turned his head to avoid the stinging spray. When it stopped, he opened his eyes again, but Ginny was gone. He looked behind him, but there was no sign of her. The glare of sunlight on the surface made the water impenetrable. Suddenly, he felt a current under the surface, and something closed over his erection. He started, then saw Ginny's body stretched out full length in front of him, her legs paddling just enough to stay where she was.

She exploded then out of the water, shaking her head and laughing. "Can't do that underwater," she said. "That'll have to wait until we get to terra firma."

Before he could say anything, her hand closed over his cock. The sensation of her stroking hand underwater was unlike anything he'd ever felt before. Then her hips came toward him and she wrapped her legs around his waist. She still had a hold on him and guided him home.

With a powerful thrust of her hips, her legs scissored behind him, she took him all the way in, letting out a soft moan. "Can you manage on one leg?" she asked, kissing the tip of his nose.

Letting his hands slide down her slippery skin he cupped the cheeks of her ass and pulled her up tightly against him. "We'll just have to see," he said.

Epilogue

It was three weeks later to the day when Vernon Settle rode into Fort Stillwell. The old man was alone, and he didn't see Slocum standing with a small group of cavalry officers. He rode with his head down, one arm limp at his side. His clothes were caked with dust, and he looked as if he'd been dragged behind a horse halfway from Mexico.

Slocum excused himself and started toward the old man as he slipped from the saddle then wearily started to loop his reins around a hitching post.

"Mr. Settle," Slocum called, "Vernon, you all right?"

Settle turned his head slowly, like a man who was too tired to listen to one more word. When Slocum rushed up to him, Settle stared at him through bloodshot eyes. Then, as if it suddenly dawned on him who was standing before him, he jerked his head up. "Slocum, where's Ginny? Is she . . ."

"She's fine, Vernon. She's staying with Colonel Martin's family."

Settle shook his head. He stuck out his hand, and Slocum noticed it was trembling. "Thank God," he said. "When I went by home, I thought . . . hell, Slocum, you know what I thought. I want to see Ginny. Take me to Ginny."

"All right. But why don't you go on in and tell Colonel Martin what happened, first? Then you can get cleaned up and I'll ride over with you."

"I guess that'd be all right." He looked toward the front door of the two-story building that housed the commanding officer's headquarters. When he tried to step up onto the boardwalk, he had to lean on one knee. "God almighty, I'm tired," he said.

Slocum led the way into Martin's office, past an adjutant who scowled when he recognized Settle, but made no move to intercept him.

Martin was at his desk. He looked up casually, finishing the scrawl of his signature with one eye still on the paper. When he recognized Settle, he slammed his pen down and came out from behind the desk.

"By Jesus, Vernon, you look worse'n something the cat drug in. Cat wouldn't even bother with something looks like you do."

"You're looking fine yourself, Charlie," Settle said. Even his sarcasm seemed listless.

"Your little girl's staying with Martha. You're a lucky man to come out of this damn-fool adventure alive, Vernon. You know that, don't you?"

"I know it. Sure I know it. But we done what we set out to do, Charlie. Somebody had to."

"What do you mean?"

"I mean we got the bastard's been selling guns to the Apaches. I think you know 'im, too." He looked hard at Martin, as if unwilling to supply the name unless Martin asked.

The colonel seemed to realize it, and said, "You want to tell me who it was, or am I supposed to guess?"

"Fella name of Breckenridge. I think you know him. Thomas Breckenridge, his name was."

"Was?"

"We hung him, Charlie. Him and his driver and two other men. Caught them in the act, we did. Giving Army-issue rifles to about twenty of them red devils, down near the border. Before he swung, he told me all about it, Charlie. Didn't need no trial,'cause he told me everything. Named names, he did. There's a few more wasn't with him, I'll tell you who they are. One's already dead. My own damn nephew. You can do what you want about the others. We cut off the damn head, so the snake'll die no matter what."

Slocum watched the old man closely. Settle seemed to be holding back on something, but it was clear he wasn't going to say much more.

Martin steepled his fingers under his chin, nodding slowly. "So that's why I was always short-shipped. The bastard was skimming guns off my shipments."

"And ammunition, and horses, and you name it. Bastard was playing both ends against the middle, Charlie. You should've known that."

"It doesn't matter now, does it, Vernon?"

Settle didn't answer right away. He looked at Martin for a long moment, then turned away. He started toward the door. Over his shoulder, he said, "Come on, Slocum, you and me got to talk about building a new house."

A special offer for people who enjoy reading the best Westerns published today. If you enjoyed this book, subscribe now and get . . .

TWO FREE

A $5.90 VALUE—NO OBLIGATION

If you enjoyed this book and would like to read more of the very best Westerns being published today, you'll want to subscribe to True Value's Western Home Subscription Service. If you enjoyed the book you just read and want more of the most exciting, adventurous, action packed Westerns, subscribe now.

Each month the editors of True Value will select the 6 very best Westerns from America's leading publishers for special readers like you. You'll be able to preview these new titles as soon as they are published, FREE for ten days with no obligation.

TWO FREE BOOKS

When you subscribe, we'll send you your first month's shipment of the newest and best 6 Westerns for you to preview. With your first shipment, two of these books will be yours as our introductory gift to you absolutely FREE, regardless of what you decide to do. If you like them, as much as we think you will, keep all six books but pay for just 4 at the low subscriber rate of just $2.45 each. If you decide to return them, keep 2 of the titles as our gift. No obligation.

Special Subscriber Savings

When you become a True Value subscriber you'll save money several ways. First, all regular monthly selections will be billed at the low subscriber price of just $2.45 each. That's

WESTERNS!

at least a savings of $3.00 each month below the publishers price. Second, there is never any shipping, handling or other hidden charges—Free home delivery. What's more there is no minimum number of books you must buy, you may return any selection for full credit and you can cancel your subscription at any time. A TRUE VALUE!

Mail the coupon below

To start your subscription and receive 2 FREE WESTERNS, fill out the coupon below and mail it today. We'll send your first shipment which includes 2 FREE BOOKS as soon as we receive it.

JAKE LOGAN
TODAY'S HOTTEST ACTION WESTERN!